BOJAN BABIĆ

GIRLS, BE GOOD

OMNIBUS NOVEL

This book was published with the support
of the Serbian Ministry of Culture and Information

GIRLS, BE GOOD

Bojan Babić

Translated by Nataša Miljković

Book cover and Interior layout
created by Max Mendor

© 2015, Bojan Babić

© 2016, Glagoslav Publications

www.glagoslav.com

ISBN: 978-1-911414-26-1
ISBN: 978-1-911414-27-8

BOJAN BABIĆ

GIRLS, BE GOOD

OMNIBUS NOVEL

GLAGOSLAV PUBLICATIONS

CONTENTS

I am myself a God in my own universe,
In this damp basement, it's raining outside,
A universe unexplored and endless and unpredictable,
A God not immortal at all.

Anastasios–Pandeleïmon Leivaditis

PROLOGUE

Dear Director Sager,

Please accept my resignation from the post of investment manager as final and irrevocable.

Before I get to the point, I would like to remind you of the short chronology of events related to my career in our company over the last several years.

It all started back on 25 December 1989, exactly on Christmas Day, when, at a short meeting at the Ministry of Education of the Republic of Serbia, formerly SFRY, I presented a prototype of a toy which, we all assumed, would be all the rage in the future globalized world. As manager of new investments, I had given up spending the holidays with my family in order to foist a small plush lemur on minor conceited apparatchiks of an anti-democratic, quasi-socialist decaying system. The lemur had flown in from Boston, picked me up here in Frankfurt, and together we went to Belgrade, the Ottoman-European town its residents love to call a city. If you remember, and I am sure you do remember quite well, the mass production of our plush toy was supposed to begin two years after that meeting, at a plant of the first German-Yugoslav toy factory to be built in Pančevo. The Ministry was supposed to issue a certificate stating that the product was useful for the education of children at an early school age, which would exempt us, as investors, from most taxes and put us on the same level with the then state-run companies in terms of privileges and subventions. In order to achieve this, I had to take the secretary general of the Ministry of Education, a certain Dragan Milanović, out to dinner. That dinner, let me remind you, cost us over thirty thousand Deutsche marks. At that time, offering a bribe was considered to be a wise business move. I was even given a pay raise for the success. I am sure you can remember this, as well.

We, self-proclaimed creative economists, planners, entrepreneurs, politicians, we all rely on statistics and research, on experts' projections. Despite this, we are always necessarily optimistic. It seems to me today, I am certain, that being objective and being an optimist at the same time is actually an oxymoron, something like being a Christian Democrat, since, you'll concede, we don't follow research and objective indices, but we want research and objective indices to follow us and our hormonal or suchlike ambition, or a consequence of an early frustration of ours. I am convinced we don't invest in the world so it becomes better, worthier and richer, so that our investment pays off, but we make the world a better, worthier and richer place because, for some reason unbeknown to us, we wish, we feel a need to invest in it. I know, my director, that it is no use lamenting over spilled beer but, you tell me, who would have thought that everything would be fucked up so spectacularly? Nobody. Neither you nor me.

Unfortunately, two years after the above-mentioned meeting in Belgrade, we witnessed a total collapse. Only the zero series of small big-eyed plush monkeys designed by the American hit-making *JoyToy* studio came out of the factory plant. Our strategic planners advised us to start with a female version of the lemur, intended for girls, as in focus groups they more easily fell for hit toys with no sign of new technology. This is why the zero series had a pink tail and made-up eyelids with which female lemurs would blink with each movement up or down. Male lemurs would follow only after six months.

Right after our spectacular beginning, the war broke out in Yugoslavia, and as a consequence of the sanctions we abandoned that market, and the lemur zero series, universally but pretentiously ironically called Aya, was on sale throughout Europe and the Mediterranean countries of Africa and the Middle East. Thanks to that idiot of a woman from the marketing department, the advertisement was utterly wrong or good for nothing. The sales were, despite the affordable price, disappointing, to put it mildly. We moved the production to the Czech Republic and there we made a boom with luminous sound-emitting plastic swords and R2-D2 robots.

The factory in which I placed so much trust had been closed down even before it started operating at full capacity. My lemurs were soon forgotten. No-one thought about them and I myself attempted to erase them from my mind. But it didn't work. The failed investment worth two million marks was my direct fault. I should have seen where the things were heading for. I should have seen what and where I invested. You generously forgave me this loss because of my previous successes and new promising plans, for which I am grateful to you, but I must say I have never forgiven myself. My motivation for work has, together with my lemurs, gone to the dogs.

Dear director, this is why I decided to resign from the post of investment manager and to move to my parents' village near Eslohe. A relative of mine will find me a convenient small property. I'll have a garden and a dog. I've had enough of everything. Life is too big for me at this time, it goes over my head. I have to carry out a tactful withdrawal for two or three years, while there's still time, and after that, who knows. I'll say it once again – this decision is final and irrevocable. I give up my right to severance pay and compensation for the unused vacation days.

The years spent working with you have been nice and difficult, as life itself. Take care.

Kristian Adler,
Former new investment manager

Kristian had written his resignation letter for the third time. He wasn't happy at all with the arbitrary tone and informal manner of address, but he couldn't do otherwise. He decided this was it. He put the paper in the envelope and left the envelope on the director's desk. He went outside. He walked down Kaiserstrasse trying not to think, possibly for the first time in the last few years, about irresistible pink–tailed lemurs. As he was further away from his company's headquarters with each step, he managed to eliminate them, at moments, from his conscience.

He didn't even suspect that the zero series – the entire small army of lively tiny pop–eyed plush animals had been taken over by a force larger than any manager, any company and any country, that lemurs were ready, at a signal, to be deployed to any position in any world, to carry out any mission assigned to them.

And their mission was larger than this world.

LEMUR THE FIRST AND THE LAST BELGRADE
(TANJA MILANOVIĆ, 8 YEARS OLD)

December 1989.

An old man holds out his hand. A hand is held out by itself. The doctor with earpieces on places the cuff of a blood pressure meter around his upper arm. The old man doesn't change the expression on his face. The systolic pressure acceptable. The diastolic pressure elevated, but still acceptable. This is only a procedure, after all. The figure of a man in a dark blue coat close by. The man's head cannot be seen. There's a television in the background. A gray screen with no moving images. The old man is sitting on a white metal hospital bed. The old man first looks at the doctor, pleadingly, then at the headless man, which spices up his pleadings with fury. Everything turns into surrender.

A woman is concerned. A thin old woman with a colorful silk scarf around her head walks to and fro. Like she is thinking, making decisions. Something between a peasant woman and a townswoman. Drained by vigor, attitude. With no make–up on. Her scarf is tucked into her fur–collar coat. It looks expensive, unlike everything else. A princess – a witch.

The old man and the woman together, in front of a low wooden piece of furniture, stare at one spot, as if avoiding seeing anything, anyone. Then they look, though. He, then she. It's not them as individuals that look, but hatred, helplessness, something that reminds of hope.

Now the two of them are sitting. At the same place where they stood, only now they are sitting on simple chairs in front of an even simpler table. Punished kids at a much too small desk in a corner. His left elbow and her right one are leaned on the smooth surface of the table so as to provide a semblance of nonchalance toward the moment. A failed semblance. Now the man is also in a fur coat, a black, pitch black one. An old black tomcat and his yellow domestic tigerish cat cornered. Sticking by their proverbial cunning, they dare not even bristle in the face of imminent danger.

Someone addresses them from aside, as if reading. A male voice, whose tone wishes to remain objective, spits out the word *executate*. The old man reacts to this by straightening his back and swallowing his saliva. He grabs the edge of his fur coat and makes a move like he wants to button up, but he doesn't. Any changes on the woman are visible only to those who really immerse themselves in the picture. She stays stiff for a moment. She doesn't breathe. She taps the back of her right hand with her left forefinger a couple of times. He reacts, though. The corners of his mouth slant downward, he gives a weird smile. The smile of anti-matter. He rises even more. He starts to talk. To talk loudly. He recalls having been listened to. Every single word he uttered. Every syllable. Shouting out, he tries to evoke those memories in the other present company as well.

But only ghosts are present.

The old man exclaims incomprehensible sentences. The rhythm is simple, repetitive, two–one–one–two, then all over again. He signals each auditory and probably semantic climax by raising his hand, and he concludes each auditory and probably semantic thesis by abruptly lowering his hand. There's nine of those raisings and lowerings. The ninth lowering turns into a strong blow on the table surface. At the same time, this puts an end to the memory of his power. The last try. His lips reassume an invisible smile of fear.

Her eyebrows hang low. Their lowness is so dominant that the tired eyes are hardly noticeable. As if she is trying to tell him something with her composure – *There's no hope. Don't you see it's all over.* Then she realizes it's all right for her to give him the pleasure of the last twitch of consciousness. Seemingly uninterested she bites her lower lip, then she licks it all over. A flicker of tragicomedy in this sight. Her beige purse suddenly finds its place on the table, but remains marginalized in front of the audience. As if nobody wonders what's inside. The purse has no role at all. Chekov's rule does not hold true for this performance.

His instinct of self–preservation still leads his words. *No* – can be discerned from time to time. No.

He raises his finger. He waves it, then points it at someone. Following this direction leads us toward another part of the room.

Finally, on that other side, we can also see the present ghosts. The ghosts are men, people in uniforms, people in old jackets, with greasy hair. There are about fifteen or twenty of them in that small room. Some of them wear green clothes and helmets, rifles hang on their backs. Out of the rifles peeks a mechanism which softens the blow to the shoulder while shooting a bullet. Rifles on their backs, in their hands. Some of the ghosts talk. Blame. Rationalize. This is visible, if not comprehensible. They explain a decision reached a long time ago. Executate.

His still raised forefinger moves from a symbolic area of threat into a concrete space of enumeration. All the while, the defense seems to take on a more detailed form than what everybody wants, the process taking place here seems to get diluted. Everybody gets nervous. They don't want to listen. There's been enough of form. The woman has already rested her cheek on her palm, her elbow on the wooden surface. She's bored. Can anyone be bored at such moments? She's really bored – there's no other word for it. Still, she is suddenly all aflame in order to crush the monotony, in order to participate. She's also had enough of form. She starts shouting, waving, darting her eyes, spitting on the present company, offending. The woman becomes an active participant. The old man calms her now. He holds her hands with his own, so they are still, decent, seemingly dignified. He steals her scene masterfully.

The ghosts take over. After all, they didn't want to listen to what they heard. Whatever might have been said would have been the same. Ghosts speak briefly and clearly. They also want to hear something like that, a brief and clear silence. And even someone who doesn't know their language could understand that the decision was important.

For a second she casts a bestial glance at them. Prompted by a hormone that tells her body *Run! Run!*, she rises but becomes aware it's only a hormone, it's nothing, she pretends to have risen only to pull the creased fur coat from under her bottom and cover her thighs with it. It's, like, cold.

All of a sudden. With no end, everything ceases. The end is not when a logical conclusion is reached, but when the time comes for lunch. Everybody stands up. They get out. The old man throws his black fur cap onto the table, having no–one else to address. Only one of the armed ghosts stays with him and his wife. And yet another one, invisible again. That one issued orders. They aren't someone to talk to. He gives an order to the armed one, to perform this, then that, to do something to them – it seems so according to their reactions. She doesn't want to. She won't part from her old man.

Then something like *Impre... Ampreun... Impreuna!**

She repeats the word persistently. It must be trusted. She presses herself against the old man, although she is being separated from him. He also pushes her away, as if to save her. Two green ghosts give in at last and they are tied together, without separation. Those are neither any kind of chains nor serious ropes, they are leashes that look harmless, but they still trigger an outburst of screams, a total confusion of being. Then more greens come close. They manage to bend the woman's hands behind her back. *No! No!* They tie him, too. He is calm and dignified. This all somehow appears to fit into his image of himself. The size. The significance. Even though this seems humiliating at first sight, probably anything less than this would truly humiliate him.

----

*   A Romanian word meaning "together".

Darkness. Darkness. Nothing. Then, inexplicably, everything changed after a few moments. The old man and his wife (an old woman?) in front of the building where the above show took place. The colors are ochre, or some kind of dirty yellow, old yellow the color of a wall, then white that frames the space around the windows and separates the yellow wall from the gray concrete, dead gray, on the floor, slightly climbing toward the walls of that building which looks like a school. Maybe a prison. School buildings are often said to have been prisons.

The old man and his wife (an old woman?) cannot be seen for more than a moment. And even at that moment, when this most beautiful prom couple is about to assume an ideal position for a photo in front of their high school, for an act which is supposed to immortalize the past – the past that is never as it really was – a shot is heard. One, then suddenly a lot of them, more than fifty.

The ghosts are the ones who shot, we decide since we cannot see them. We can only see the smoke. The smoke prevails now in this gloomy exterior. A more observant eye can see that it's the dispersed dust from the façade into which innumerable bullets buried themselves.

A pause. Silence. The ghosts wait. Perhaps they are thus slowly becoming humans. A cloud of dust floats in the air, as if the particles lost their weight. This human dust of death and the space dust of life shackles history, for ten seconds or for eternity. Space gets involved in the hiding of the crime, of the criminal.

In the end, the dust settles after all and an eerie sight comes into view.

A stream of blood leads the eye toward what used to be a woman, an old woman, now merely a loose structure that holds an expensive fur coat, giving it some kind of volume. The wall behind her is totally riddled with bullets.

He is on the right, the old man.

His body, kneeling down, then leaning backward, is in such a bizarre position that it looks like a fallen scarecrow. Those knees that slip into the foreground, and those feet spreading below the thighs... they are almost funny, grotesque. Because this corpse seems to be showing his genitals to the world. *Here you go!*

Still, when you look at his upper part, you can see that the black fur coat is all unbuttoned and that it has fallen onto the ground, and out of it sprout his chest in a suit, then his neck and head, slightly thrown back and half–turned to the left. An attitude full of significance, an attitude in which national heroes' torsos used to be sculpted.

They are no longer together. Impreuna. She bleeds, dead. He strives heroically, a cadaver.

Deus and machina. Snow covers the wide screen. Buzzing.

Tanja rubs her eyes and averts her gaze from the disturbing sight. She sees a big mirror on the wall that was to her left, and sees herself in it – a short eight–year–old girl in a tracksuit and woolen socks, lying face down in front of a TV table and holding a remote control so firmly that the sides of her fingers are completely red. Too tight a sight.

Sprawled on a soft tufted carpet, Tanja doesn't understand the play she is watching, but wishes for it to continue. She wants to see what happens next. Somehow she expects it to have a happy ending.

The picture gets fixed on its own. The revolution carries on.

The mesmerizing, deadly view is usurped by two men – a soldier and a doctor. They are here to check and confirm the truthfulness of execution. We realize the show isn't over after all. And it's a successful show, such that at least for a moment convinces us we aren't at the theatre, such that we believe in, at least for a short while. A formal confirmation of death is stronger than death itself.

Just for the sake of it, they feel the pulse of what used to be a big woman. They slightly lift her and immediately lower her, not gently at all. They throw her like garbage. This is merely a stop on their way to the still big man. They swiftly walk toward him. We can only see their legs, as in old cartoons. The soldier wears long black boots. He feels the old man's pulse in a somewhat comic manner, touching his forehead. This isn't enough. The doctor lifts the dead head. It is so heavy that it falls from his right hand. This head falls in a very significant, unforgettable way, as if it were the fall of a world, a god, a devil, it falls like the head of a man in the final stage of drunkenness. Blood appears everywhere. That's it. It's all right.

Tanja can hear some steps, and then the door being opened. She presses the red button, which turns off the world. The *Telefunken* television fails to switch off. Tanja presses harder and harder, all the while gnashing her teeth. She fights this monster with the intention of taming it and producing a gray surface on the screen. She doesn't succeed. Something is wrong with the remote control. Again she glances at the mirror. She sees herself. A drop of blood trickles out of her nose. She sniffs it in and lies down, wanting the one who's coming to think she is dead.

A tired grayish man on the threshold of his fifties approaches her from behind. It's Dragan Milanović, a man, a teacher, a father. He turns her around. He lifts her falling head. Still, blood peeks out from her nostril.

– *What's that, Tanja? Your nose bleeding again?*

Tanja says nothing. She tries not to breathe.

– *Tanja!*

Dragan talks to her, seemingly worried.

– *Tanja, what's the matter?*

Tanja says nothing.

– *Tanja, you aren't breathing. Oh no, what shall I do now?*

Dragan smiles, then starts touching her ears, her hair, her neck. He squeezes her nose several times. He tickles her stomach and armpits.

Tanja stiffens her every muscle. She stays strong.

– *I have to give first aid. Reanimation.*

He unzips her tracksuit top, lifts her T–shirt and bares her chest. She feels his cold hands on her skin. Using only three fingers, her father begins to press the area above her small heart. The pressure is rhythmic, weak and hardly noticeable. Tanja restrains herself from laughing.

Although the pauses between the pressures last only a second or two, these seconds seem much longer to Tanja. In order to remain in the position of a dead person, she silently repeats the verses she has learned by heart from a book she has read several times after sneaking out of her bed at night and going downstairs to her father's library.

Girt with a boyish garb for boyish task,

Eager she wields her spade: yet loves as well
Rest on a friendly knee, intent to ask
The tale he loves to tell.

Rude spirits of the seething outer strife,
Unmeet to read her pure and simple spright,
Deem, if you list, such hours a waste of life
Empty of all delight!

– It's no use. I have to apply mouth–to–mouth resuscitation.

He bends down to her face. He presses his lips against hers. Tanja can feel the touch of fat, dried and cracked skin. Tanja can smell stale tobacco. She can smell alcohol.

He brushes her lips.

She moves back a few centimeters, then returns. This time he kisses her longer, over the mouth, cheeks, nose, eyes. He rubs his beard shaved yesterday against her neck. As the air shrieks passing through his withered alveoli, he exhales his breaths into her chest, her stomach.

Tanja doesn't move.

Dragan pulls out the end of the elastic ribbon stretching around Tanja's waist, then he pulls her bottoms down. He slips his hand into her panties.

Tanja comes to life at last. She smiles.

– You're alive, after all.

Father stands up and kisses her again, this time on her hair.

– Your nose is bleeding again. Too much?

– Only a drop.

– I've brought you something. A present. Look.

– What's that?

– A monkey. A lemur. This is a prototype. Do you know what it means? That you are the first in the world to have such a toy. The first.

– It's nice.

– Come, be good, say thank you to your dad.

Tanja hugs her father. Father lifts Tanja and places her in his lap. Tanja is in her father's lap. The lemur is in Tanja's lap. Tanja is comfortable. Tanja tries to change the channel.

– Leave it, let me see what is happening to Romania.

– Who is this man who's been killed?

– Nobody. Nobody. In fact, we'd better not watch.

Dragan lifts Tanja. Dragan lifts Tanja and the lemur. With his left hand he gets hold of a small bag he has brought with himself. Dragan and Tanja and the lemur and the bag go down the stairs into the subterranean room. The subterranean room is the library.

– I've brought some new books for the library.

– Let me see.

– Never mind. They're still not for you.

Dragan locks the library door. Dragan, with Tanja in his embrace, passes by Aeschylus and Euripides and Sophocles, Cervantes, Rabelais and Grimmelshausen, Flaubert, Huysmans and Gide, Tolstoy, Dostoyevsky, Mann, Musil, Vuk and Branko and Dučić, Rastko, Andrić and Krleža... and Ben and Trakl and Brecht... and Rilke and Pound and Brodsky and Mandelstam... and Céline and Hamsun and Nabokov... and all the other men. He passes and sits down in his reading chair. Again he places Tanja in his lap.

– Kiss your daddy.

Tanja kisses her father. With his finger, father wipes the red drop above her mouth, then he licks the drop off his finger. Father lays his hands on Tanja's hips, on Tanja's thighs. Again he slips his hand into her panties. They both shiver with pleasure.

A stream of blood on television. Dead–gray wall. Ghosts. Since they cannot be seen.
  – Do you love your daddy? Say you love your daddy.
  – I do.

  Executate.

LEMUR THE SECOND
THE OUTSKIRTS OF CHIŞINĂU
(JULIA, 12 YEARS OLD)

Look at me, Julia. Look here when I tell you!

Right.

Good. Look here. Now come a bit closer to the camera. Move your hips, as we said. Right. Smile. Blink your little eyes a bit.

Okay.

Why did you stop? Shall we turn up the music? This mister will do it straight away. Is it all right? Do you like this song? You do. Bravo.

Right. Twist a bit, like at a discotheque, to the rhythm. Bravo.

Strut your stuff, as models do. Want to be a model? Why did you all stiffen up then? Yesss.

Now, like, your strap has slipped off your shoulder. Not that one, the other one. It's slipped, like, accidentally. Riiight.

Now take off your undershirt. Not so fast, slowly. First touch yourself on the stomach a little, like you hesitate. You see you know. Lift it a few centimeters. Drop it. Lift again, higher. Hesitate. Smile.

Now take it off completely. Leisurely. Turn your back to me and throw the undershirt onto the bed.

Stop! Don't turn around yet.

Unbind your hair. Cover your breasts with your hands. And now turn around. Right.

You're so beautiful... Yes, yes.

Now remove your hands. Drop one, put the other on your neck. Dance a bit more again. Raise your both arms. That's right.

You're alone. You're free. You feel great. Want to turn it up more? There you go. Now kneel down on the floor. Toss your hair to one side. Put your hands on the floor. Now come to me on all fours. Look at the camera like there's something sweet there. That's right. Seductively. Good. Now turn on the other side. Your sweet little bottom to the camera! Move it back and forth. Left and right. Put your hand on your bottom.

Caress yourself a bit. You know how. Like in that movie. Bravo. You're enjoying it. Are you enjoying it?

Well, you are, you're enjoying it.

Now pull your panties halfway down your bottom, only halfway! A bit less. Stop. Move them back, then all over again. Only halfway! Riiight.

Close your eyes.

Touch your thighs and your bottom a bit more. Touch your titties with the other hand.

Strut your stuff. Strut your stuff well! More! Touch yourself a bit more. That was good.

Open your eyes.

Take off your panties. Lie on your back. A bit to one side. Your head a little to the right.

To the right! That's left. Ah, good. Bend your knees and join your legs. Get it? Yes. Bend a bit more. Fine. Look at the camera. Send a kiss to the good guy who's shooting.

One more. Enjoy yourself.

Put your head back again. Toss it. Put your hand on your thigh. The other hand. The other thigh. Yes!

Move your hand up and down, up and down. Down. A bit more down. Right to the pussy. Stop there. Stop for a moment! Don't move.

Is it good like this? What do you say? It's good. A bit more, huh?

Julia! Turn your legs a bit more toward me. Yes. Caress your thighs again as a moment ago.

Is it tickling? A little, isn't it. And are you cold? A little. Nothing serious. Nothing.

Great. That's my good girl.

Now that boy comes through the door, and you are, like, surprised because he's caught you. Get it?

Like he's caught you red–handed. Can we do that? Come on. Wait. Wait, not like that. Good, you are surprised, but don't look like you're afraid. Like, you're surprised, but you also smile a bit. Like, you're naughty.

Come on again.

Let the boy sit next to you. He's brought you that toy, the monkey. Isn't it nice? Yes. Take it. Feel free to take it. Now let the boy touch you. Gently. Good. Look him in the eyes and smile more. Kiss him on the cheek. That's right. Now look down at him, at that thing. Come on, come on! It isn't funny. Look down there and stop clowning around if you want us to go home soon.

Goddamnit! Julia! Be good! Get serious.

There you go. You see you know. Leave the toy. Leave it. You'll take it later. Now unbutton him. Aha. Mhm. Ah, he could have put on some pants with a zipper. Now she's gonna unbutton him for half an hour. The child is confused. Can you, Julie?

There. Bravo. My sweetheart. That's right. And now, do you know what you are supposed to do? We've talked about it. Put your hand around it. Then up and down. That's right. Uh, what do you say, like a grown–up woman! Now a bit faster. Look him in the eyes. Down again. Again in the eyes and smile.

Down again.

Now lick it. Aha. Put it in your mouth. Aha. See how my Julie knows everything she needs to know. A bit more, just a bit more, Julia. A bit faster. You see how the youngster enjoys it. A bit faster. What do you say, she seems not to need my instructions any longer. Over.

Did you record everything properly? Okay? Yes. Here, wipe yourself.

– *Mum, was I any good?*

Super.

– *Can I go for a shake now with Anna and Victor? You promised.*

You can, just wait for the mister to give us the money.

– *Shall I take that monkey?*

LEMUR THE THIRD
KARMIEL, GALILEE, ISRAEL
(ALMIRA, 14 YEARS OLD)

– Almira, it's time.

Composure is the only visible thing on the wrinkled face of an old man who, below himself, on the branches of his luxuriant family tree, has seventeen children and more than fifty grandchildren. She is one of them. Six months before the action, girls spend most of their time with their spiritual elders and they are completely isolated from their family during the last four days. It's a rule, but in this case Almira's spiritual elder is her relative as well.

Today she feels it her duty to be composed. To be happy and alive at last, because she is already in heaven.

Two women take her to a special room, separated from the spacious cellar hall by white curtains. A few spasms unsettle her stomach and then her feeble hands, after they've taken her household garments off her body.

Lives, people, wars, all have the plural, all are hellish. Peace is one. Peace, she says to herself.

They bring close to her bare untouched waist a women's belt, prepared in advance, four flat boxes attached on the inside, each filled with a hundred grammes of semtex, a plastic explosive which could, in this quantity, blow two passenger planes to pieces. The plastic has already been mildly warmed with hot towels, so it doesn't cause discomfort to the young skin.

Almira shuts her eyes for a moment and then she quickly remembers that she must show wavering on no account, that she must have no qualms whatsoever, because she does not even know how to doubt, since no one has taught her so. She is more determined than ever.

Thin cables leading to the triggering mechanism pinch her in the region of the stomach. Skilful and experienced hands pass over her stomach and back muscles, connecting everything that needs to be connected. They touch her tenderly, blood rushes to her nipples, which become stiff. She begins to breathe deeper and faster. This kind of excitement is unfamiliar to Almira.

That's it, she thinks. An invitation to heaven. That's what my body is telling me.

One of the women orders her, quietly and seemingly disinterestedly, to get dressed and hands her a gray skirt and a white shirt. In the school uniform the girl appears again before her elder relative, who kisses her on the forehead, placing a leather bag with books on her shoulders, and with an unearthly authority utters a non–question:

– *Do not forget. They are occupiers. All of them. You know what you're supposed to do. There. Be a good girl.*

She nods her head, rushes to her desk, taking a small toy from under it, a plush lemur, and goes out into the street full of children dressed the same.

This is her first day in a new, experimental, bilingual, mixed school, designed for common schooling of both Arab and Hebrew teenagers. Teaching is performed in both languages and history lessons are separated. The rest is the same for all students.

She enters quietly and occupies a seat in the third row. Beside her is a girl with a nose piercing, Sara.

After several lessons and two short breaks of awkward introductions, Sara gets to learn about Almira everything she has been taught in case she is asked about her family, what she likes to eat, listen, watch, read, wear. Almira's Hebrew is modest but sufficient.

At the same time, Almira gets to learn about Sara all truths which would otherwise remain hidden if it were any other girl, because she talks about some things no-one else would on a first encounter, about her being a child of rich parents, a year older than the others, intelligent, but a repeater, because she is undisciplined, going away on unannounced trips, on her own, in obscure company, a garrulous whore, which is how she jokingly calls herself, about where she goes out, about sleeping with a guitarist of the local band *Hatred* last year, about having an older boyfriend, and about them gathering and drinking and smoking weed in an empty, never–populated building. As soon as lessons are over, she goes right there and then on a further jaunt. Her new friend must, simply must, accompany her too. Almira manages not to respond to the invitation and after the last bell she simply leaves the school together with Sara, walking by her side, wherever she would take her. Almira looks at the city as if looking at the world for the first time, in fear and hidden curiosity. Around them walk bodies, not people.

And one should feel scorn for the body and its calls.

One should feel. Scorn.

One should feel.

Almira foolishly follows her new guide. Almira finds herself in a two-room apartment crowded with young people. The majority of them are in their late twenties. They hold cans of beer in their hands. Between their forefingers and middle fingers are cigarettes and marihuana. They grow longish curly or apparently sloppily cut hair on their heads. In their heads they nourish speculations about freedom. Some of them harbor some more talented and less stereotypical thoughts. There are a few foreigners there – Americans and Europeans. They use their longest, pre–university vacation for exotic journeys across Eastern Europe and safe regions of the Middle East. Smoke. This is a place where prejudices about youth consciously come true.

Fifteen minutes later, in a corner, Sara is kissing a boy who seems to be smiling for no reason. On the stage contrived out of small crates, boys and girls appear in turns. Holding a small microphone before their mouth and clumsily following song lyrics on a fifteen-inch monitor, they sing current world hits. Tones are computer-generated, almost intolerably reduced. No-one seems to mind this.

A shortish eighteen–year–old is verbally most dominant of all. Suddenly he approaches Almira. He hands her a sheet with a list of tracks.

– *Choose.*

Without questioning herself whether it's obedience, which is only familiar to her, or something totally different, Almira points her finger at one of the songs.

The boy takes her by the hand. He brings her to a platform and tucks the microphone in her hand. Almira is a queen.

My loneliness is killing me...

She's good, really good.

The crowd turns to listen to her. Even though most of them don't like the chosen song, her rich voice is supported by mutual singing, whooping and jumping to the rhythm.

They sing along:

... I must confess, I still believe.

I still believe!

And she feels something akin to freedom. She starts to sing more loudly.

She lifts her hand, waving to the rhythm, as some of her predecessors used to do on this throne. She shakes her hips.

Precisely at that moment when she abandons herself to the surroundings, she feels something under her wide shirt detach itself from her skin. It starts to glide down her back and stomach.

Trying not to draw much attention to herself, halfway into the song she calmly leaves her performance and rushes out in light steps.

Dark descended over the earth long ago. It's overcast. Sounds of crickets are intolerably dull. Almira walks toward a wide deserted street which seems to be leading nowhere. With the fingers on her left hand she forcefully clutches the small plush lemur.

From the apartment she has just left, the voice of youth can still be heard, accompanying the melody...

... I still believe!

The following day people woke up with coffee and newspapers, which said that on Golda Meir Boulevard a woman suicide–terrorist activated an explosive device and that there were no other casualties. The minister of the military stated that terrorist attacks had to cease and that the armed forces would take any necessary steps to let the masterminds of violence know that the state would not tolerate the slightest incident endangering its citizens.

Retaliation pending.

Wars have the plural. Harb. Houroub.

Peace is one. Peace. Salam.

LEMUR THE FOURTH
FRUŠKA GORA, SERBIA
(ALEXANDRA, 13 YEARS OLD)

She sits in the park, crying. She doesn't know why she's crying. A mustachioed statue of a hero climbs down off its pedestal to her, sits beside her and kisses her on the forehead, then kisses her on the mouth.

The teacher calls her to the blackboard and tells her: "Solve this equation". The sum is easy and she knows the answer, but she has a bird's claws instead of hands and so she can't hold the chalk. She wants to tell the teacher that she can't hold the chalk, but instead of a mouth she has a beak and she lets out a bird's squawk.

Now it's night–time. She stares up at the sky. The moon is revolving quickly around the earth, faster and faster until it eventually falls down to earth, but everything is all right, because her grandma brings her a basket of cherries.

Then she feeds mechanical iron pigs, and they sing her a lullaby, all in the same mechanical way. They lick her feet with their mechanical tongues. They scratch her.

Now she is towing a ship across town with her hair. Then she is chased by babies in the street, and she's naked. That's what Alexandra's friend Maja dreams, strange things, crazy things. Every morning Maja comes to school with a new story. Alexandra listens and says nothing. She says nothing because she dreams of nothing. She dreams of nothing because she hardly sleeps at all. No sooner does she fall asleep than she is woken by a noise, disturbed by light, disconcerted by fear. And if she is fooled for a moment by her forcibly closed eyes and begins to dream, the dream is always the same. She is at lunch with her family in a nice large house, it's their house. She reaches for the salt, and another hand smacks her lightly, because salt is forbidden. A stupid dream – and boring, above all else.

And then, at that moment, Alexandra always wakes up.

That's the only thing she dreams. And she only sleeps for a short time, a couple of minutes, and then comes back to reality. She lies in bed, in the dark, for hours on end, all night long, with a blanket over her head, and hugging a toy, a small plush lemur.

It's the same every night. Tonight is no exception. Then suddenly the light comes on.

– Get up, son, come on. It's already half past four. We're going stalk. You didn't forget, did you? Come on, come on. What we've been hunting so far is nothing compared to stalking.*

Once you've tried it, you'll be asking to go again and again. Stalk hunt is the ultimate way to hunt roebucks. You know, a true hunter-stalker must be in good condition, know the ground and game excellently, have a sense of ease of movement and be fully observant. And we have

------

*   When they want to show affection, fathers in Serbia and the Balkans sometimes call their daughter 'son'.

these qualities, don't we, son? For me, stalking, this hunting pursuit, is a real art.

To approach the quarry, the superior ones, to find yourself in a position to shoot, or to test yourself, and then to slowly get closer to young herds, not yet good for shooting, to examine the limits of nature, your own nature.

The chase gives you so many opportunities to improvise, to use quick thinking and such suspense as you can only imagine, which is the sweetest thing of all. Adrenalin surges at every step as you stealthily get closer to the animal.

And when a buck you haven't noticed up 'til then rises from the grass. Pleasure. Stalking. Pleasure. Nothing's better.

Come on. I've got a .243 Winchester for you. OK? I think it's the right size for you now. You're ready for it. I know, I can see what you want in your eyes, but you're still a beginner. No rush, you'll get to the .222 Remington. It's for the experienced. You still have difficulty carrying it, but you'll grow. You'll get stronger. You will, my son. You will. I'll keep it, for the time being.

And I've seen what you draw all the time, in secret. Nice gun stocks, rifles. Shooting. Targets. I too like to see pretty, engraved weapons, choice stocks, the glow. But you should not yearn for such things. Engravings do not shoot the game, my son. What is important is that the rifle does the job. And that it is suited to its owner, while the engraving – the engraving may be over–done and become kitschy. What I used to see all over Greece and Turkey, those guns and rifles, yes, all that looked like mockery. As if a rifle were entertainment for lonely spinsters. As if it were some kind of embroidery or tapestry, or something. Engravings all over weapons with no order or plan, meaningless, shapeless.

Come on, get dressed.

Alexandra pulls back her covers. Alexandra takes off her pajamas. Alexandra is in her underwear. He's looking at her, stern, but proud.

– *Come, my son.*

Her legs are muscled, strong. Her body is robust, sturdy. She is wide, not tall. She isn't fat, you couldn't say that. Once she heard her relatives describe her as well–built.

Her father taps her on her behind to hurry her along.

– *Come on, son. The quarry won't wait for us.*

Alexandra hastily puts on a khaki uniform and cap. There's no time to wash her face or for other morning rituals. To catch the first ray of sunlight. To seize the day and draw it close. To catch a perfect roebuck and shoot it right below the shoulder blade. Killing with a single shot – the first commandment of hunting.

Off they go. They're jolting along in a white Lada Niva on the muddy roads. They breathe in the woods. They stop. They search. Search without success. Oak trees, long grass, ditches, brooks, foxes' dens, abandoned cottages, pheasants, wasps, all flash before their eyes for two hours until it's time for breakfast. The secret is to be patient, to persevere. To take more time than the roebucks do. To always be one step ahead. To be a human.

Jolting along in the Lada again. Deeper into the woods. The road tapers off into nothing. On foot. They search. And search. Their boots pick up turf, mud. Their feet become stronger. Wider. He is in front, some twenty steps. He's a scout. He spots something. He freezes to the spot. He quietens Alexandra's footsteps. He kneels down behind a tree stump. She lies on the ground, in a ditch. He observes, motionless and silent. He doesn't talk. The silence lasts a minute – an eternity. He points his finger and whispers ecstatically, at the top of his voice, so Alexandra can hear him over in the ditch.

– I can see him. There he is. About a hundred and fifty meters away, I'd say. He'll come out into the open. He'll come out. Come. Come on, boy, walk into our sights. That's right.

What's the matter now? Why are you standing, my boy? Come on, feel free. We mean you no harm.

Just to have a little fun. Ahaaaa. A plane flies by. Ignore the plane, little buck. Just go on your way. To the water. Come, come slowly.

Can you see him, Alex, huh? See how handsome he is. Nature is a miracle. God is great. What perfection He has created. Look at those horns. They'll be yours, Alex. Are you happy? Yes. You're happy.

The roebuck approaches, no longer afraid.

– That's right. Come now, Alex, shoot. Breathe in, just like we practiced. Gun stock on the shoulder. Find him. Can you see him? Yes? Good. I have him in my sights too.

Look him in the eyes. Aim for the heart. He can't be just wounded. Under no circumstances. Right through the heart, under the shoulder blade. Then he's dead in an instant, in no time at all.

I love this moment. Alex, this is what I live for.

That's it. Two hunters. One target. Both have it in their sights. That's how a special connection is created. I couldn't feel it with just anybody, you know.

Alexandra aims. She looks at the animal walking freely across the freshly mown grass, directly toward the river. The river is between her and the animal. Father is on the same side of the river as her. Father. Alexandra turns with her eye on the sight. From the animal's head to the man's head, to her father. Ninety degrees.

What this right angle covers: mossy tree trunks, ferns, tree stumps, a small metal pot, a puddle with the surface covered in pond scum, a starling, spring. Nature through the blur of rapid movement. A face; an expression of tense exaltation.

Through the visor Alexandra observes the man aiming at the roebuck. She takes a deep breath and with a tranquil, so very tranquil micro–movement she points the little cross at the line of his temple. The man talks passionately:

– *Only with you, Alex. With you. Because you are the best. You are my own creation. No–one else could share this love of hunting with me. No–one else could understand me. You are so young, and so... Ah, my son, you still don't know what people are like. Not yet. And it's better to stay that way. Animals are better. Much better.*

Alexandra aims at his temple.

– *Look at those eyes of his. Huge.*

Then she lowers the visor to the speaking lips. She'll blow them up. She imagines them blown up by a gunshot. Flying lips. Speechless. He's mute. Mute. At last.

He says:

– *Look at him, look closely.*

She's looking at him, closely.

– *How carefree he is.*

Despite a spasm of passion, she recognizes light–heartedness on her father's face.

– *He doesn't even realize you have him in your sights.*

She smiles at the thought that her father wouldn't even think she has him in her sights.

– How old would he be? Five, probably. He must have lots of young. You see, Alex, how God has arranged it. Animals pass away, disappear, and their young go on living. Fending for themselves. They don't suffer, they don't grieve, they don't wait for forty days, six months, a year. And us, how closely related we are. You see, if I wasn't alive, if I disappeared, if someone, for example, shot me accidentally now while hunting, what would you do? How would you cope? I shudder even to think.

Alexandra puts her forefinger on the trigger. She clenches her teeth.

– Here he is. He's moving. Good boy. There. Just a bit to the left. Turn a bit more to the left.

She lowers the gun aimed to the left, to the neck. She's focused on the jugular.

– There. That's the ideal position, Alex. Got him? If so, shoot. Shoot below the neck, near the shoulder blade. Shoot for the heart.

She lowers the sight further, to the chest. The heart.

– Don't wound him. Kill him straight off, with one shot. Don't torture him.

Go ahead, shoot.

He makes a move with his body as if he wants to step away from his rifle and look at his daughter.

Alexandra briskly resumes her initial position, with the weapon pointed at the five–year–old roebuck. Father glances at her expectantly.

– Go ahead, now. Shoot. He'll run away.

Without hesitation, Alexandra fires a bullet, then one more. The buck takes a step in fear, then falls down. He tries to get up, but falls again. He raises his head, then lowers it. He keeps on moving his legs, then stops. He lets out a cry.

– You've wounded him! You've only wounded him. I

should have known you weren't ready. Let's go over there. Come on now. Quickly.

They run across the brook and undergrowth. They approach the quarry. There's a big gaping wound on a leg muscle. Blood. The buck screeches. Cries out. The screeching is unbearable. The woods echo. Father positions himself over the fallen buck, observing him, not without pleasure.

– Look at him. He's hiding his eyes. He's staring into the ground. Look, Alex. That's how all of them look at the ground. They pray to it, or whatever. Praying for a miracle. How pitiful they are. How we used to slaughter them. Killed hundreds of them. And they all hid their eyes from death in the same way.

They were all the same. They repented. Groaned. Squealed. Repented, not because they knew they'd sinned, but because they hadn't moved, escaped in time. Fools. A lowlier species. Animals. They are animals. Worse than animals. Ha! Shoot now, Alex. Finish the job. Come on. Be good. You have to do it. Right in the heart. Lean the rifle over here.

How he screeches, wounded, he moves his lips inwards, draws them in. His gums are visible.

– Go ahead. Shoot!

Alexandra feels dizzy. Alexandra feels dizzy.

– Shoot. Shoot! Shoot! Shoooot! Kill him. Be a man. A man, Alex. Shoooot!

Alexandra finishes the job. She kills the animal. Straight in the heart. The last jerk. The last. She can feel her father's hands on her shoulders, his lips on her eye.

– That's right, my son. I'm proud of you.

As he hugs her, he pushes her head under his arm. She can smell his sweat.

– Now you're a man. Now you're a man, my son.

Alexandra cannot sleep.

She lies in bed, in the dark, for hours on end, all night long, with a blanket over her head, hugging a toy, a small plush lemur.

Alexandra cannot dream.

LEMUR THE FIFTH
THE MEDITERRANEAN
(SAMIA, 6 YEARS OLD)

– What's your name?

   – Sonja.

   – What kind of name is that?

   – Italian.

   – And you're Italian?

   – Not yet, but I will be when we get there.

   – All right, when we get there. But what was your name before, back at home?

   – Samia.

   – Well, that's a nice name.

   – I don't like it.

   – Sonja, are you afraid of water?

   – Not really.

   – Do you think I wouldn't dare to jump?

Five thousand two hundred and sixty meters deep, between five and twelve million years old, forty–six thousand kilometers of seashore, an area of twenty–five million square kilometers, known as the Great Sea in the Bible, or simply the Sea.

The centre of the old world, surrounded today by twenty–one countries: Spain, France, Monaco, Italy,

Slovenia, Croatia, Bosnia and Herzegovina, Montenegro, Albania, Greece, Turkey, Cyprus, Syria, Lebanon, Israel, Egypt, Libya, Malta, Tunisia, Algeria and Morocco.

– You think I wouldn't?
– I don't know. I believe not.
– It's high from here, but I'd dare.
– Not that it's high, but it's scary. The waves.
– I don't care. I can swim well. I learned when I was a little boy, in the Medjerda.
– But this is different.
– Why?
– The sea is large.
– The sea is water and a river is water. One and the same thing. Water is water.
– This water is salty.
– So what? It's even easier then. Salt makes water denser, so it's easier to float on the surface.
– What do you mean by dense water?
– It's dense and it's easier to swim in. When it's light, you quickly sink into depths. That's what I mean.
– And it's cold.
– Never mind. I'll cope.
– But do you know how far land is?
– What do you think?
– It must be a kilometer away.
– And you know how much a kilometer is?
– It must be the width of the Medjerda, twice as much. And a bit more, surely.
– Once I swam across the Medjerda to the other bank, and then swam back. There!
– I don't believe you.

– You don't have to.

– All right, but there are fish down there.

– In the Medjerda as well.

– Medjerda, Medjerda! But these fish are big and dangerous. For example, the shark and the killer whale.

– You think there's the killer whale here?

– Yes, it lives in the sea.

– No. It lives in the ocean.

– Well, this is actually an ocean.

– No, this is a sea.

– Ocean.

– Sea!

– Ocean!

– Let's ask someone older.

– I won't.

– Why? Let us ask.

– I won't ask anyone older. Let it be so, the sea.

– You don't believe me, but I tell you, the sea.

– Never mind, all the same, you'll drown.

– I won't.

– You'll die. You'll drown and get chilled and frozen and you'll die.

– I won't.

– You'll get frozen and die and fish will eat you. A shark and a killer whale.

– Well, what if I die?

– It's sad when someone dies.

– It isn't when I die. I'm not afraid of death.

– I don't believe you. Everyone's afraid of death.

– You believe nothing.

– I don't believe this.

– I'm not afraid to die, really. Why should I be afraid?

– Well, when you die, you no longer exist.

– It isn't true, you go to heaven.

– It doesn't matter, you're no longer here. Wouldn't you be sorry for not being able to do everything you wanted because you died?

– No.

– I am sorry when I think like this.

– I'm not. I won't do anything.

– Tell me another! There's plenty you could do in your life and you won't do anything at all?!

– I won't. What I've been doing so far is enough. I've ridden. A horse. When I was at my uncle's in town. He's a policeman. He sells oil with some friends. I rode in his BMW. He asked my dad if I could stay with him, but dad didn't let me. He says we're proud. We'll go to Europe, Paris. We don't need you. Dad says that my uncle is bad, for kids. But he let me do anything. I even tried beer. But don't tell anyone. My uncle let me. I've done everything. I won't do anything else.

A transport ship, around ten years old, although it looks much older. Fifty–nine and a half meters in length, about eight in width. A vast space on the lower deck occupies most of the area. The richer are on the lower deck, those from towns who know the carrier, their families and friends. Hundreds of people packed on the upper deck and in the narrow passageways on the side. Closely packed against one another, they can neither sit nor stand. They find themselves in awkward positions, half–asleep, breathing, awaiting morning, for anything to happen. Among them, leaning against the railing, legs outstretched, hanging over the water, are two kids. They attempt not to meet each other's eyes while they're silent. Then, still, they cast a glance at each other.

– *Have you ever had a girlfriend?*
– *What do you mean?*
– *I mean, have you had any?*
– *Yes, I have.*
– *You're lying.*
– *I'm not. Uncle took me once to a house where there were only women. And there a woman caressed me while he was in the room. Her name was also European. She's my girlfriend.*
– *She isn't your girlfriend. You cannot even remember her name. She's a whore. You've never had a real girlfriend, one who loves you.*
– *None of your business! It's my business whether I've had one or not.*
– *Which means you haven't. You see, I knew there was something for which you would be sorry to die.*
– *Will you be my girlfriend?*
– *No, I won't.*
– *Why?*
– *I don't fancy you.*
– *Come on. Then I'll know I've done what you say I should do. In my life.*
– *But how?*
– *Simply, let's kiss.*
– *I won't. I won't. I'll snitch on you to my mum!*
– *Where's your mum?*
– *She stayed on the shore. There wasn't any room this time, but she'll come on the next ship. I must wait for her.*
– *Come. Let's kiss. Come, be a good girl.*

– I won't, see how many people are around. They'll see us.
– They won't. Everybody's asleep, and it's dark.
– I won't. There's a million of them. Leave me alone.
– All right. All right.

…

– How long is this ship going to stand still?
– I don't know. A short while, I guess, until dawn.

The two children try not to meet each other's eyes. They are silent, as the others.

The silence is broken by a rhythmical sound of a machine. There's some light approaching from the sky and a strong wind awakes the densely packed throng. A helicopter hovers around the vessel, making uneven scattered waves. It descends to about ten meters above their heads. Packages of various sizes are being thrown out of the aircraft. "Aid! Aid! Food!" in Algerian and Malian dialects. All food aid falls on the front part of the deck. There's a commotion, a rush for the first food they've been given over the past three days, which is how long they've been circling round the territory of free waters. They all rush one over another, all of a sudden everybody lets out loud cries, breaking the silence, the death. All the crowd moves to the north part.

The boxes are being torn into pieces in the first seconds upon fall. One of them falls directly into the boy's hands. He tears it apart and starts to examine its content: bandages, wet wipes, pressed food, sandwiches, energy bars, soap, a diaper, toothpaste and a brush, a sanitary towel and a toy – a small big–eyed lemur.

The lever of fate moves forward. The front, north part of the ship, tilts slowly under the pressure of the crowd, sinking into the water, whereas the back part, relieved now of the emigrant weight, rises. The helicopter disappears in the distance. The panic of hope caused by the arrival of aid turns into a pre–death panic, a fleeing–back.

People break elbows, knees, necks, women scream. Waves get larger.

The boy kisses the girl.

The vessel tilts to a side. The vessel sinks.

Swimmers start to jump out. Non–swimmers stay until the end.

The salinity of slightly over thirty–six per mille. The average temperature of thirteen degrees Celsius. Very small concentrations of biologically important substances make this sea oligotrophic, barely productive. It is, in a sense, the victim of malevolent geographic destiny, relatively deep, of a small area, too north for coral reefs to grow in it. Also, there are no underwater valleys, and the seabed in shallow coastal waters plunges to the depths of a thousand meters or more. The land on the coast is as barren as the seabed, and due to such geographic characteristics the Mediterranean Sea accumulates large amounts of pollution. For this reason, in the second half of the twentieth century the Mediterranean is spoken of as a sick sea.

The boy hands the toy to the girl.
Do you like it?
No, it's scary. Its eyes are scary.
Never mind. Take it, as a souvenir.

OK.
Let me tell you something. Sonja isn't an Italian name.
But?
Russian. I think.

LEMUR THE SIXTH
VIENNA
(HANNAH, 10 YEARS OLD)

Hannah, I've brought you something, a surprise. Look, it's a lemur. See how nice it is? How big eyes it's got? It reminds me of you. It's yours. Always carry it with you, let it keep you company. You're so beautiful together.

Hannah, I have to read this to you.

Mind you, Hurricane Katrina hit New Orleans.

A huge hurricane came from the shores of the Bahamas. It hit the American soil near Miami, then it reached New Orleans with devastating effects. Severe damage in the coastal areas. Eighty per cent of New Orleans is underwater. It also took its toll in the American states of Alabama, Tennessee, Georgia and Kentucky.

A thousand eight hundred and thirty–six people died, seven hundred and five were reported missing. This is said to be the costliest natural disaster in the United States ever. Billions of dollars.

Take a cookie. It's nice. You'll lick your fingers.

A storm surge caused strong erosion of the soil and coastline, in some cases a complete devastation of coastal areas, five hundred and sixty square kilometers of the land turned into water surface. Imagine how much that is! Marine mammals, brown pelicans, turtles and fish lost their natural habitats and breeding grounds. The storm caused the leakage of twenty-six million liters of oil. An entire town flooded with a mixture of water and fossil remains, oil. Disaster.

See, Hannah, my sweet little Hannah?

Do you understand how lucky we are?

Are you aware of the fact that the average temperature has increased by almost 0.8 degrees in the twentieth century? More in the last hundred years than in the previous ten thousand years. And by the end of the twenty-first century it will have increased by at least two more degrees. The sea levels have risen. It's a madhouse outside.

Hannah, take a cookie. Take it, take it. With honey and walnuts, as you like it.

And listen to this. More than forty people killed in two suicide attacks at underground stations in Moscow this morning.

The attacks were carried out by two female suicide bombers. Hey, women! The first explosion occurred at seven fifty-six in the morning, on the train that stopped at Lubyanka station, near the headquarters of the former KGB. What does that mean?

Thirty minutes later there was another explosion at Park Kultury station. In the first attack twenty-two people were killed, twelve injured, in the second attack twelve people were killed, seven injured.

You see. For example, I leave in the morning to buy some groceries at the Naschmarkt, go underground and take the U–Bahn, and there it goes, a bomb explodes and kills me. It tears my body into pieces, never to be put together again. It kills me, Hannah. And what happens to you then? Do you ever wonder? No?

Terrorists. They make a bomb in their houses which can demolish a whole neighborhood just like that. The world is rife with them. No–one is safe.

Hannah, do you understand now why I don't let you move from here?

Hannah, realize once and for all. I won't explain it to you any longer.

Look, it says here what's happening all around. In Croatia, which is near, four minors killed themselves. There is some doubt that it's the work of the Sect of the Black Rose. The Black Rose is said to gather together people with the darkest affinities, mostly young, who conduct most obscure rituals serving their lord, the Evil One. They are Satanists, they love the devil instead of God.

Can you believe it, Hannah?

Eat that, sweetheart.

They meet in some suburban houses in Europe, America, Australia, and Asia as well, in groups of about twenty people, they utter incomprehensible words, conduct various rituals and organize sexual orgies. I've even heard that a collective rape of a sixteen–year–old girl has taken place. Above all, those Satanists offer sacrifices to their devilish lord and in the process, of course, they drink the victim's blood. It even happened that, a few years ago, for Easter, they sacrificed a four–year–old child to the Evil One. Most often they woo naïve girls and boys around schools and at clubs, in the evening.

And you wanted to go to school. Like all I say is nonsense. Like I don't think about you and I am not giving you proper education here.

Hannah, this is for your own good. There's nothing for you outside. You see, now you have a lemur, too.

You know yourself that your skin is sensitive. See how white you are, the sun will burn you.

I have to tell you this.

There are some children, people. They are called angels, there in Africa. I fear for you, that you'll become like them – those white little Ethiopian albinos. They're cute, but if they go out in the sun, their skin gets burned. They start disintegrating. You know what things they're doing to them, there in Nigeria. They persecute them, because they have white skin and blond hair, but black parents, and they're afraid of them.

Come on, be good, eat those cookies.

The time will come for dinner and you haven't finished your lunch yet.

They are considered to be ghosts, witches, there in Africa. People think they should be killed, so they slaughter them brutally. They take out their bones, dry them and break them into pieces, chop them up, turn them into powder. Then they drive out evil spirits with the angel's dust. This is what they do, those sorcerers, there in the Sahara. I know, what they do isn't good, but this should be known. You have to remember that.

I have a geographical magazine with an article about this on several pages. There are some pictures, too. Just have a look. I'll bring it. Learn that article by heart, and I will ask you to talk about it later. This is good for you.

Hannah, are you hungry?

Hannah, shall I bring you some meat, you aren't eating anything.

I've prepared some steaks. With cheese. The way you like them.

I'll go and fetch them for you.

And you read about the albinos.

Off I go.

Wait, wait. What's this now?

The border has faded away?

I haven't noticed this before.

Did you touch anything, Hannah?

Did you go outside the lines?

Uh?

I hate to beat you, you know. I hate to tie you. How can I put it into your head that you have nowhere to go outside?

Didn't we talk? Didn't we agree? Mum worries about you. Mum goes everywhere so you have everything. You don't worry at all. You are here, in our world.

Remember this well, I'm telling you this for the last time:

Europe. Austria. Vienna. 154 Baumgasse. Apartment number 21. Room to the right from the hall. A circle one meter in diameter drawn with red chalk next to the left wall.

It's your world there. You have everything there.

And you go nowhere. Never.

Hannah, put it into your head for once!

There's no other way.

There's no–one.

There's nothing.

There's nothing that isn't in this circle.

There's nothing!

LEMUR THE SEVENTH
TIKRIT
(RUKIA, 7 YEARS OLD)

All clear.

All clear.

Who are those individuals on the corner?

Hotel Two Six! This is Crazy Horse One Eight. Can you see those individuals east of our position? I think they're armed.

Affirmative, we can definitely see 'em. There are three or four of 'em. Yeah, definitely four. Here's another one. Five.

Are they armed? You have a better view, Hotel Two Six.

Affirmative, one is armed. And another. Yeah, they have AK–47s. I'm not sure. It seems so.

Fuck it, I'm not sure either. I request permission to engage.

Wait.

The individuals are moving toward the entrance to the building. They are crossing the street. I request permission to engage.

Wait. We have to receive a definite confirmation that they are armed.

We'll soon lose sight of the individuals. I think we have no–one on the other side at the moment.

Roger that. Yeah. You're the closest. Just make sure they're armed.

Do we have permission to engage?

Okay. You have permission to engage. Over.

Copy. We're ready to move. I cannot approach 'em now. They disappeared behind that building. They're fucking fast.

What's that one holding? Is that an RPG?

Aha. We've got an individual with an RPG. We have to shoot.

Wait. Wait. We'll approach from the other side.

Hotel Two Six. We don't shoot until we have a clear view.

Copy. Okay, Crazy Horse One Eight. We're waiting for a good position.

What's this? Is one of 'em cocking his weapon? I can't see well.

I'd say he's cocking it. What poor visibility, damn it! Shit!

Don't panic. Just be fast. Can you see 'em well?

Now we can see well. They turned round the building again. Did he shoot? Shoot from the RPG?

Hm, it was unclear. I thought I heard something.

Keep looking for an ideal position, Crazy Horse One Eight.

Okay. We're flying to the north.

And don't request permission again. As soon as you have 'em within sight, fire.

I surely will.

Go a bit more to the north. Even more.

Here we are.

Say when you have 'em within sight. Wait for a clear situation.

I've got 'em. I have a clear situation. I'm shooting.

Go ahead. Fire. Light 'em all up! Let nobody escape. Come on. Shoot!

They're running away.

Shoot! Shoot! Come on! Right! At everyone! That's right! Keep shooting. Don't stop. That's right.

Okay, we cease. Hotel Two Six, we cease the fire.

Okay. Do you have them all?

Yes, we engaged all five individuals. Wait. There's another little bird fleeing. We're shooting. We're still shooting.

Fuck it, Kyle, don't let him escape.

Hotel Two Six, the bird seems to have flown away. Did you see him?

Crazy Horse One Eight. I think he's injured. He crawled behind that white van. He's definitely there. Over.

Copy. OK. I'll prepare a position for engaging the van.

Affirmative. Open fire on the vehicle.

Did he have any weapons?

Affirmative, definitely. All five of 'em were armed. KIA, then RPG and AK–47s. I'd say so. We can logically conclude that there are some weapons in the van. Doubt rational. Action justified. Now shoot.

There you go. We engage the van. We'll neutralize the last individual.

This is Command. This is Bushmaster. Hotel Two Six and Crazy Horse One Eight, did you engage all armed individuals?

Affirmative. Final and definitive affirmative.

OK. Hotel Two Six, go down to your positions if Crazy Horse has definitely finished his operation. Go down to the ground, take photos and give a report. Over.

Copy. OK. We're going down. Crazy Horse, can we go down? Have you finished your operation? Are we safe?

Affirmative, Hotel Two Six. There's no–one else down there.

We're going down. Location Main twenty. We're going down slowly. Are we safe?

Affirmative, Hotel Two Six. You're safe.

Look at 'em. Dead animals.

Beauty.

Yes, ha–ha, beauty. L'art pour l'art. A good shooting. You've fucked 'em all.

Thank you, Collegeboy. You know how to pay a compliment.

We're going down to the ground. The exact location of the bodies: Mike Bravo five–four–five–eight–eight–six–one–seven. That's the street, the crossroads next to the parking lot. In front of the parking lot. Aha.

There's one further down. He's crawling. He's wounded. He's crawling. Can you see him from above? There, he's still behind the van. He's creeping.

Affirmative, we can see him. He's crawling. Is he armed? Can you see any weapons?

Negative, not yet.

Come on, boy. All you have to do is lift your weapons and save yourself the trouble. Come on. He's turning. Here he is. Are those weapons?

I'd say so. You open fire from the air, and then we'll approach.

Okay, we're firing. Firing. We've lost him in the dust. Fuck it. We can no longer see anything from the dust.

We can see. That's right. He's done. You can stop. He's definitely done. We'll approach him now. Over.

Copy. Hotel Two Six, you can approach him. All clear.

All clear here, too. The ground forces can engage. Is it okay for the ground forces to engage, Bushmaster?

Affirmative, surely. You have permission to engage, Sandglass Eleven. Finally. Over.

Copy. Okay, we're coming to the scene in armored vehicles.

I think you've just run over a corpse. Watch out a bit.

Have we? Bullshit. Fuck it. Pardon.

Oui, pardonne–moi. We're there. Getting out. Do we have permission to get out, on the street?

Affirmative. All clear. What do we have down there? Speak.

Aha. One, three, four bodies. Yes, and another one next to the van. Five bodies.

Weapons?

We can see no weapons. Only cameras, tripods. Something for recording.

What about KIAs, then RPGs and AK–47s?

Nothing. Only one camera. Tripods, two of 'em, and that's all. Like they're from some television, journalists, cameramen.

Fuck it. Screw it. It's okay, people. They knew they shouldn't have gone out. Shit happens. Cool down.

Okay. What else is down there?

There's a van, too. Wait, wait. Ambulance. That's an ambulance. That's the van. As far as I know these signs.

All right. Was anybody inside?

Negative. Everything's empty. The cabin is empty. We'll look at the back.

Go ahead, Sandglass, look and off we go from here.

Wait. We can see someone here. A patient is on the bed.

Really?

Yes. A girl. She was on a drip. Like she was supposed to be taken somewhere. To a hospital.

So, what do we have down there, Sandglass? Just quickly.

A female body. Enveloped in fire. Seven or eight years old. Her health record is still here. I don't know their letters. Collegeboy, you know Arabic. What does it say? Rukia Zaidi, seven years old. And a diagnosis. Appendix. Burst. What a nice toy she has. Simon, is this a lemur?

Yes, I'll take it for my daughter, she'll like it. She doesn't let it go, she's holding it with all her might. She's dug her fingers in. Come on, girl, be good, let the monkey go. She won't.

Didn't you tell me you had no children?

She won't let it.

Leave that. So, a female body about seven years old. Nothing else. Officially and definitely. Over.

Copy. You've been down there long enough. Make a record of everything and get away from there. Over.

Copy. All right.

This is Bushmaster. Hotel Two Six, Crazy Horse One Eight, Sandglass Eleven, you've done a good job.

Thank you.

Thank you.

Back to the base. Over.

Copy. Here we go.

Out.

LEMUR THE EIGHTH
VATICAN CITY
(FAUSTA JESUS, 9 YEARS OLD)

We fared very cheaply.

Our budget was almost unaffected.

And it was...

It was...

Wonderful.

Boris and Marta are in Rome for the first time.

A low–cost company. An affordable double room at a hostel at Piazza Dante. Second youth and first freedom. A small, smaller and smaller world. This is what brought these tough forty–year–olds to the city of captivating architecture, history woven into everyday life, to this confluence of culture, beauty and human openness.

It's spring. The last week of the month. Boris and Marta, holding a tourist brochure and a camera, wait for the red A underground line at Vittorio Emanuele station.

It's very crowded, as if the whole world swarmed to the same place they were headed for today.

They count together: one, two, three, four, five, six, seven, eight stops to their destination – Musei Vaticani.

It's spring. The last week of the month. And entrance tickets to the Vatican Museums are free of charge the last week of each month.

Boris and Marta exit the underground and walk along a wall which encloses the museum complex. The queue, composed of all ages, religions, races and ideas, is immense, stretching at least a kilometer, or two, up to the entrance into St Peter's Basilica, and further on.

Be that as it may, Boris and Marta will first visit the central part of this miniature country before they start a slow advance toward the Sistine Chapel.

Boris and Marta pass a rigorous control of Swiss Guards.

Boris and Marta are in front of the magnificent building.

Boris takes a photo of Marta from below, trying to capture the balcony on which the Pope comes out to greet thousands of exalted people. Marta clasps her hands in prayer slightly ironically in order to show her attitude toward the Catholic Church in general. Ironically, but cutely, without sarcasm. And then they go through the Door of Death – the far left entrance to the church, nudging their way through the other tourists in front of Michelangelo's statues and under the grandiose frescos. They spell out the inscription on the wall:

TIBI DABO CLAVES REGNI CAELORVM.
(I GIVE YOU THE KEYS TO THE KINGDOM OF HEAVEN.)

Some women in jeans kneel down in the confessionals. Boys leave the secret rooms with priests. This attracts attention.

All in all, it's nice, but a bit boring. After all, they're here because of the Sistine Chapel. Therefore, they get out and stand in the immense queue composed of staggering people, as if they were waiting in front of the entrance to a gas chamber.

It's boring. Travels are boring. Strenuous, in fact. Memories of travels are what we travel for.

Staggering himself, Boris takes out his small new tablet, unlocks it and goes on the Internet. Now is the right time to read the news he has missed in the last five days.

Bush's watch has been stolen.

Sarkozy says: We'll crack down on scum!

Elton John has married his partner.

Fossils found in Africa challenge the theory of evolution.

Only three hundred Siberian tigers at large.

Vatican has excommunicated a Brazilian girl... read more.

Click on more.

The Vatican has officially stood up for excommunicating from the Catholic Church a nine-year-old girl, Fausta Jesus, who was raped and later had an abortion.

A high Vatican clergyman has approved of the act of excommunication for the mother and doctors of the girl who was subjected to abortion after she had allegedly been raped by her stepfather.

Cardinal Giovanni Battista Re, head of a large diocese of the Catholic Church, has stated for yesterday's *La Stampa* that the twins who the girl carried had the right to live.

"This is a miserable case, but the true problem is that the conceived twins were innocent individuals who had the right to live and mustn't have been eliminated."

Re, who presides over the Bishopric Committee for Latin America, adds:

"Life always has to be protected. Journalistic attacks on the Brazilian church are unwarranted."

A week ago, the archbishop of the Brazilian state of Pernambuco, Jose Cardoso Sobrinho, proclaimed the excommunication of the mother who permitted the operation and the doctors who performed it for fear that the insufficiently nourished girl might not survive the complicated pregnancy with two fetuses, as well as fearing for the girl herself.

"Divine law is above human law. And in such cases when human law is opposed to divine law, human law has no worth," said Cardoso.

He also explained that the accused stepfather wouldn't be thrown out of the church. Even though this person committed "an atrocious crime, abortion – destruction of innocent lives – is still a far more serious issue." Battista Re agreed with these words, concluding that an abrupt termination of pregnancy was nothing but the destruction of an innocent life.

Journalists have even reached a priest from the village where Fausta lived. He claims to have heard about the whole story in good time, and to have tried to influence the girl by telling her to be a good Christian and not to succumb to her mother's persuasions to have an abortion and thus become a killer. But the influence of the Antichrist mother was evidently stronger than his advice.

Boris switched off his tablet. He saw a girl of mixed race in front of him in the queue, playing with her toy. It was a tiny, big-eyed lemur. The mixed-race girl pulled her father's sleeve and, in a language unknown to Boris, insistently asked: "Are we there yet?" Dad only smiled. He caught her under her armpits and lifted her. She kissed her dad. This was universal communication.

"We're almost there."

Boris feels Marta's narrow palm on his shoulder. Suddenly a massive murmur of disappointment is heard. The gate of the Vatican Museums is closed. You can enter only until one o'clock on Sundays. Who is late has to come tomorrow.

But the next day Boris and Marta were already drinking their espresso at a café at Fiumicino Airport Terminal 3, waiting for flight 442.

It was really nice in Rome.

We've never seen a more beautiful city.

The best food is on the other side of the Tiber.

And everybody drinks wine. Wine. Nobody drinks beer.

And everybody mooches cigarettes on the streets.

We've taken loads of photos, you'll see.

The best food is on the other side.

LEMUR THE NINTH
MARSEILLES
(ACHILA, 13 YEARS OLD)

The backs of these hands. The backs of these hands are so ruined. All these decades. Age spots. Fingers become stiff, bent. They turn numb more often and for longer. The skin is dry.

As the teacher watches his hands and their backs, a blonde girl utters the sentences she does not care about:

The aristocratic class of the French society was composed of the nobility and the clergy. The nobility lived off feudal lands. The aristocratic class of society also levied revenues from the complex civil service and pensions which the king distributed to the clergy and the nobility as the ruling classes. The lower nobility was, according to their wealth and reputation, considerably below the high nobility, but they also kept their feudal rights and privileges.

– That's right, Babette. There was yet another class in France before the Revolution. Which one? Who can tell me? Blanche? Tell me what you know about it.

Those were peasants and common people. They didn't have any privileges, and differed according to their wealth and reputation. Peasants represented the most numerous group of that class. Although they weren't legally bound to the land of their lords – nobles and clergymen, they were burdened with large feudal dues. They gave a tenth of their produce to the church, and paid huge taxes to the state. Their dissatisfaction was widespread and they desired the abolition of feudal relationships in order to become the owners of the land they cultivated.

– That's good, Blanche, good. Who belonged to the middle class? Why was the middle class dissatisfied? Who will answer? Achila? Let's hear you.

That's... That's... The middle class... It's...

– Go ahead. We're all waiting for you to remember. The entire class. Nothing, huh? Where's the text I kindly asked you to bring today? You don't have it, of course. But that's why you have this on your desk. What's this? A toy. What animal is this? A monkey from where you come from? Stop laughing down there. It isn't funny. We have patience for you who come here, Achila. Our city is full of your history, your religion, your minarets. Wherever you turn, your customs, your scarves, women. It's fine with me, but then I demand that you learn the French history, too. It's essential. These are basic things. That's also for your own good. I'll keep this monkey of yours until the next lesson and then I'll examine you again. I'll give it back to you only if you learn the lesson on Pre-Revolutionary France. I expect you to be good and to know this better than Babette and Blanche. And to write two pages about Robespierre. Agreed, Achila?

Yes.

– In fact, this homework is for everyone. A paper on Robespierre for Monday.

The bell. The teacher rushes to his room and locks himself in. He looks through the window at the students leaving the school. They are leaving without knowledge.

They are leaving not wanting to know all the people they are indebted to. The teacher lifts the plush lemur and tells it:

The Incorruptible, oh my Incorruptible, can you see this?

We wish in our country that morality may be substituted for egotism, probity for false honor, principles for usages, duties for good manners, the empire of reason for the tyranny of fashion, a contempt of vice for a contempt of misfortune, pride for insolence, magnanimity for vanity, the love of glory for the love of money, good people for good company, merit for intrigue, genius for wit, truth for tinsel show, the attractions of happiness for the ennui of sensuality, the grandeur of man for the littleness of the great, a people magnanimous, powerful, happy, for a people amiable, frivolous and miserable; in a word, all the virtues and miracles of a Republic instead of all the vices and absurdities of a Monarchy.

That's what you used to say, my Incorruptible, when you were building our France. And today. Look at them.

The teacher turns the lemur toward the window. Together they look at large young steps into nowhere. Then there appears Achila. She's tall and heavy–set for her age. Her jeans are tight around her fresh hips. Her face is round and young. Her shoulders are tanned. She isn't dressed at all in accordance with the culture she comes from. She smells so different. She smells of cocoa, of young cunt. You can see this. Her smell can be sensed even from here. The teacher unzips his trousers. He clasps his penis firmly with the soft lemur in his right hand. He starts masturbating, delighting in the naked Arabic navel liberated in the free citizens' republic. As Achila waits for her transport, shifting her weight from one foot to the other, the teacher whispers:

Vice is Cain's stamp of aristocracy. In a republic, vice isn't only a moral and political crime. A man with vice is a political enemy of freedom.

Oh, my Incorruptible!

Principle is above all.

Right. Oh, Achila! Just a little faster.

Democracy is a state in which the sovereign people, guided by laws which are of their own making, do for themselves all that they can do well, and by their delegates do all that they cannot do for themselves.

Oh, my Achila. Listen to me. Listen to what I tell you. Feel me. Feel where I touch you.

The main weapon of a republic is terror. The strength of a republic is virtue. Virtue – since without it terror is fatal, terror – since without it virtue is im…potent.

Achila, no!

He pauses for a moment. He glances at his hands again, his fingers. They're so ruined. All these decades are visible on them. Age spots smile at him from the back of his hands. The pause lasts for two or three seconds, and then he goes on.

It still isn't the right moment to think about years, though they are in abundance.

No.

No thinking about years yet.

No. No thinking yet.

No.

No.

No.

Yes!

Yes!

Come on! Come on! Achila, come on!

Faster, Achila.

A bit faster, Achila!

It's still no use thinking and talking about years. And when, my Incorruptible, when, when fatigue rules over us and when we already have them in abundance. That time will come only when we start dying.

Oh God, how old these hands are. Wrinkled, with white speckles. And these age spots.

Three drops of sperm slowly trickle down the lemur's cheek.

Oh, my Incorruptible. You see, I am like you.

No–one helps me.

I come across conspiracy all around.

LEMUR THE TENTH
THE VILLAGE OF SEMINOVO,
SMOLENSK, RUSSIA
(SOFIA, 13 YEARS OLD)

Peasants.
Narrow minds.
Idiots.
Dead men.
Haters.
Beggars.
Mob.
Blind men.
Mice.
Dung beetles.
When you spit, you spit on yourselves... What do you know!

Sofia repeats this crying, as she holds the wheel of a twenty–five–year old Belarus tractor with both hands and all her might, and with her right foot presses the gas pedal which reacts to pressure only if superhuman violence is applied to it. She drives toward the main and only crossroads in the village. In the open trailer there's a gravestone with a name written on, not inscribed (since no stonemason agreed to carve that name, at any price) and an improvised coffin made of boards.

You know nothing!

Sofia repeats, looking right through her tears.

The road. Mud. Wide tire tracks. Potholes. Mud. Cats crossing. The dark. Then the dim yellow light of the old–fashioned streetlamp. A ditch by the roadside. Magnificent concrete railings and decrepit fences. The school she goes to, every day, except the last few. The church. The shop. The hay. Curtains down. Potholes. Remains of snow. Mud. Wide tracks. Cats crossing.

To the left and right of her view of the glass surfaces of the tractor cabin, articles from daily newspapers and gossip magazines are stuck so they can be read from outside, with these headings and sub–headings: the alcoholic Victor Istinsky has raped, then murdered a boy and disappeared; the whole village chases the rapist; the monster caught; is this a man or not; reinstate the death penalty; death would be minor revenge; the freak got what he deserved; God's hand reached him in custody; autopsy says a heart attack; the village won't bury the maniac; people are buried at our graveyard, not animals; he doesn't deserve a Christian burial, etc. The door hangs loose on the frame of the tractor cabin. The window is cracked. Papers flutter in the draft. From the roof, on a thin string, hangs a toy she got from her father three years ago, a plush lemur with captivating eyes. It's spring. It's still cold, but Sofia isn't.

Leaned on the piss–covered wall of a closed inn by the road, two workers from the road and sewerage company of the Pochinovsky region wait for Sofia. She's phoned them for urgent intervention, claiming to be her own late mother, promising them a triple wage if they agree to drill the asphalt at three a.m. in the village, kilometers away from their headquarters.

Mum doesn't feel well, so I had to come. Here's the money, don't you worry. Just take this off the tractor.

The men in orange uniforms and thick coats, one of them forty years old, something like a boss, in charge of getting the machinery out without any notice and using it for personal profit, and the other, a youth, with still open eyes that naively say *you'll see, I'll dupe you all,* glance at each other questioningly. Once they make sure the money is here, they take the big coffin off the trailer and negligently throw the marble stone on the ground.

What the hell is this?

Nothing. You'll drill here. Here!

Sofia draws two lines in the dust with her foot and makes a cross in the middle of the only crossroads.

Here they come every morning. To gossip. Now they'll have something to talk about. Come on, start the drill.

Not knowing what to do, the younger man holds the Hycon asphalt hydraulic drill and looks at the other as if waiting for what that other one, the boss, will decide.

What do you want, girl? To drill in the middle of the crossroads at this time?

You just do what you're told. You'll be paid.

And what do you have in this coffin?

No, leave that! It's none of your business.

The younger man understands the boss's silence as a sign of approval and drags his hellish contrivance over to the marked spot. The older one utters through his teeth:

Just be quick.

He fears the reaction of the peasants, who will certainly wake up.

The noise that the hydraulic drill makes at night in this countryside wasteland is many times louder than in a modest urban wasteland, in which it is softened by the sounds of cars, machines, people, civilization – no–one even notices it there. But here, with the first crack in the asphalt, the first light appears at a window. It is immediately followed by another. In five minutes the dozen neighboring households become awake and watchful. Everybody observes, but no–one dares go out, so the hole in the road gets larger and begins to look like a tomb. Sofia doesn't find it necessary for it to be deep. Half a meter of dug earth beneath the thin layer of the asphalt is enough, as well as thirty centimeters of the earth above the deceased, so everyone can see. Everyone. Even if he is later removed from here. It's enough for everyone to see, for the burial to take place, in the middle of the village. In front of everyone's house. Newspapers might report about it. If they did then, let them do it now.

Hey, girl, are we burying someone here?

Sofia takes out more money and stuffs it into the younger man's pocket.

Finally, a first house owner runs out in front of his house, leans against the fence and observes the situation. He is followed by other peasants, too. The loudest begins to speak:

Hey, what you are doing, men?

The workers shrug their shoulders and look at the girl.

Hey, girl, Victor's daughter, what are you doing? Are you burying your old man in the middle of the village?

For god's sake, men, get rid of that drill. Don't pretend to be crazy. Leave that girl alone, she's nuts like that old maniac of hers. How did she talk you into drilling in the road?

Women rush to the crossroads. They punch the workers. They seize their tool, shrieking and waving their hands. Their husbands seem to calm them down, slackening a bit. Some get this idea and tear a board off the coffin in which Victor lay. In fact, it was only his body there, but for those gathered, it was him.

Laths, spades, anything that was within easy reach, fly toward the body. Even the shiest ones come together because of the hubbub and attempt with all their might and all possible means to receive a second helping of divine justice. A ritual murder of the murdered.

The older worker drags tearful Sofia aside so as to save her from sporadic assaults.

Listen, when they cool down, I'll take the body and find a rightful place for it somewhere.

Good. I'll find some more money.

It's just that I don't want money for this.

His hand fell on her breasts.

You know, I want something else. Only if you can be good and keep silent. And only if you're ready for it.

I am.

He takes her into a small yellow communal service car.

The road. Mud. Wide tire tracks. Potholes. Cats crossing. The dark. Then the dim yellow light of the old–fashioned streetlamp. A ditch by the roadside. Magnificent concrete railings and decrepit fence. The school she goes to, every day, except the last few. The church. The small shop. The hay. Curtains down. Remains of snow. Potholes. Mud. Wide tracks.

LEMUR THE ELEVENTH
THE VILLAGE OF ZAWIYAT, EGYPT
(ZAYNAB, 11 YEARS OLD, HAFSA, 7 YEARS OLD)

Hafsa, I won't let you go. Don't go. I won't let you!

I was also sent for when I was your age, to visit a woman, they said, who would do my hair because it was disheveled. Mum came along, too. And grandma. And aunts. They wore hijabs, but I would have a new haircut, like the actress Anushka on TV, I thought.

I also meant to tell them to leave only this part on the back, and to cut the front, so Husani would like me.

They took me far away, over there behind that large house of old Kafele, the blacksmith.

I hurried along, pulling their hands. I wanted to see. I'd never been so far away from the village.

Then they pulled me aside and took me into a room. The dark.

When a lantern was lit, an old woman was there, a granny. "Naya, Naya!" It was Naya, a nanny, they told me. There was goodness in her eyes. I was happy because she was the one to cut my hair. Only mum had cut my hair before, but now I would be especially pretty.

Naya caressed my hair. Her fingers were shriveled and tender. She was all wrinkled. She looked the same as we imagine old women in tales.

It was misty and warm in the room. It was full of some kind of vapor. I was sweating as aunt and grandma started to undress me. I was left only in my panties. I thought this was how it should be. Mum smiled, but looked at me as if she was afraid.

Then I noticed a large bathtub in the corner. It was half–full of hot water. Naya poured some more from a jug. Then aunt took my panties off, as well. It was a bit funny to me, but I didn't protest. I thought they would bathe me and wash my hair before they cut it. This was the right order, I believed.

Before they led me into the tub, Naya pulled my legs apart, this much, and started to touch me all over, on my stomach. Then, on my thighs. Then she took a jar with some herbal ointment out of a drawer and rubbed it in between my legs. You know, on my pussy. There, right there.

Then she moved aside, along with mum, aunt and grandma. They whispered something there, and they seemed to put something into her hand, which she stuffed into her pocket.

Ten minutes passed and I started to feel numb down there from that ointment she'd applied. Naya pinched me and I hardly felt anything.

Naya took me by the arm and motioned me into the tub. I stepped in. It was hot, but I wanted to do everything properly.

As I sat in the tub, aunt approached me from the left, grandma from the right, and mum from above. They caressed my stomach and thighs, and then slowly spread my legs. Mum caressed my head. It was pleasant.

Naya appeared again, with scissors in one hand and a folding knife in the other. Mum put a cloth to my mouth and closed my eyes with her hand, and then pressed my shoulders with her whole body so I couldn't move.

She whispered into my ear:

This is how it should be, Zaynab. Be good, Zaynab.

Naya then muttered not to worry and that she would finish shortly.

I felt numb down there. I did, but still I felt it when she spread those lips down there and pressed the cold metal of the knife onto my skin. I felt it. I tried to break free.

Naya pulled something out with her one hand. She pulled hard at me down there, but in that upper part, above where we pee. I shrieked and tried to free myself.

Then she ordered mum to tie my mouth with the cloth. Mum refused at first. Then she approached me and tied my mouth as I screamed to myself.

Mum trembled and started to cry. She repeated:

Be good, Zayaib. Please, be good. This is how it has to be. All of us have gone through this. It's tradition. Be good, Zayaib.

The cloth was wet and it dripped into my throat as I pressed and bit into it.

Then I felt Naya cut something down there.

I prayed for her not to kill me. I tried to get away as much as I could, but aunt, grandma and mum were strong, so strong. Naya was placing the blade for a long while.

She made a cut. Down there, somewhere close to the inner lips. Then she swore, as if she'd done something wrong. Then she pulled me again, placed the knife faster and made another cut.

It wasn't supposed to hurt me, because of that ointment, but it did. I thought: this is how it hurts an animal when it is slaughtered. That's why it roars so loudly. I thought: I am also being killed.

Then Naya took the scissors. I couldn't see that because my eyes were covered. I could only hear the snapping of their blades. She placed them where she'd made the cut a moment before and pressed them quickly.

I thought I would faint. I prayed to faint, but I couldn't.

Naya turned around and left. Aunt and grandma released me. Mum still held me tight for long. I couldn't join my legs.

When she finally released me and stood up, I opened my eyes and saw blood gushing from inside me into the hot water. It was horrible.

Then all three of them lifted me and wiped me with wet cloths. They put something cold and soft down there, then bandaged my legs, left me lying and told me to relax and that everything was good.

Naya kissed me on the head as she left, smiling and saying:

This is a big day for you. Now you can get married.

And when they brought me back home, mum kissed me, crying and laughing, and telling me not to move my legs. Not that I could. They were tied to each other. And she gave me a toy, this big-eyed monkey. It scared me at first, but I like it now. I've got used to it.

Dad wouldn't even get into the room.

It stung, so much.

I lay for days on end. Do you remember? This was why, and not because I poisoned myself with the old falafel.

We all lied to you.

This was what they'd done to me. I won't let them do the same to you, Hafsa. I won't let them cut you.

They'll take you out of the house and tell you nice stories, they'll tell you this has to be done and that all of us have gone through it and that you'll be beautiful and tall if they do this to you and that the women who don't undergo this are witches and that everybody hates them.

You see, do you believe me?

You see, that's why I've dug this hole for you.

No–one knows about this place at all. No–one can find you here. And if you hear they're looking for you, don't let your voice be heard.

Here's food and water for you. It's enough for three days. Here's also a monkey to play with. It's a lemur. It lives on Madagascar. When I got it, I talked to it. I told it everything. I no longer do this, but it's nice. It'll keep you company.

Take care, Hafsa, and be good, don't say anything. Keep silent.

I'll cover you with branches. Don't worry and don't move from here. I'll visit you several times a day.

Don't worry at all.

LEMUR THE TWELFTH
ŽEPA, BOSNIA
AND HERZEGOVINA
(ALENA, 13 YEARS OLD)

Claudia Schiffer, Cindy Crawford, Linda, Naomi… on satellite TV.

Kate is being waited for, Kate is the best, outside all those stupid trends, but still inside them. Kate Moss. An unsteady gait. As if she were about to fall any moment, yet so attractive, so light on her feet.

Here she comes. Materialized spirit. Beauty that cannot be comprehended by everyone. Beauty that everyone comprehends is no beauty at all.

Kalashnikov, Thompson, Heckler, there, in the suburbs. Sporadic shots from the distance.

There's fear only when there are people. When you are alone, that's freedom.

Alen is finally alone and free.

Mother tries to buy some food, at the market, from house to house, probably with no success. Father is somewhere. Somewhere, because the times are terrible, as neighbors say.

Sister went away five days ago and hasn't come back since then. The only thing she's left behind is her room, with lots of clothes and make-up. And a small round mirror on a stand, a mirror that magnifies the face of the viewer and the model.

Alen is alone. This is what he likes most. When he's alone, time doesn't exist for him.

He opens a box wrapped in a decorative paper and takes out tweezers. Hair by hair, he plucks his slight, just grown mustache, until only smooth skin, reddened from so much pain, is left in its stead. He calls to mind some advice for teenage girls he's heard on television. One piece was this:

How to apply make-up?

Corrector. A corrector should go in two colors. The first is necessarily one shade lighter than the skin and it covers smaller spots and softens shadows under the lower lip, around the root of the nose, under the eyes. And then a yellow corrector. It covers acne and redness.

Of course, only one corrector lay hidden in the box, but it was enough for such a young face. Alen covers the newly formed redness on his mustache, as well as a few pimples on the nose.

Foundation. After the corrector, apply a liquid or cream foundation. Take special care of the area beneath the jawbone toward the neck, around the ears and the hair root. In these parts only spread the foundation which is already on the face for consistent tone.

Done.

Blush. It would be ideal for light brown blush to go from the earlobe, diagonally down to the corner of the mouth. The cheekbone is thus pronounced. Ordinary peach or pink blush should be applied on the cheekbone itself.

There's no blush. But a mere carefully rubbed lipstick spot will be of use.

A seductive look. For a look that will seduce any boy, you should encircle the eye with an eye pencil. Start from the inner corner of the eye, then draw it right above the upper lashes for the full length, and then along the lower lashes. Before this, it is necessary to sharpen the eye pencil well. For a catty, seductive look, join the eye pencil at the lacrimal glands, then make a slight arch downward, and in the outer corner an arch upward.

Alen swiftly runs into his room for a sharpener and sharpens the edge of the eye pencil which can barely be held between the fingers since it's long been too short to be conveniently used.

After this, apply a lighter eye shadow from the lashes to above the middle of the eyelid, but not under the eyebrow, so as to make an impression that the eyes are bigger than they actually are. Then apply a darker eye shadow from the outer corner of the eye toward the middle. This way. Also apply the shadow right under the lower lashes.

Fusillade happens more and more often. Shouts. Swear words.

A beauty gradually emerges in the mirror. Beauty is all wisdom. Wherever you set from into the adventure of thinking, eventually you get to beauty. Beauty is the end of any philosophy and any faith.

Mascara. Apply the mascara in several layers. Don't forget the lower lashes and emphasize them with at least one layer.

Eyebrows. Start drawing at the level of the nose root. The highest point is the line that joins the nose root to the pupil. Finish at the line that joins the nose root and the outer corner of the eye.

Now, the mouth. You kiss with the mouth. It's the most sensitive part, the most important to Alen. This is why make–up should be applied to it with special care.

For full lips, first of all apply a thin layer of foundation, and then draw the contours with a pencil. The pencil is placed on the edge of the mouth or right below it, like this, and never above the edge. Only then does the lipstick come. Apply it with a brush, and then press a tissue against the lips. Gloss comes at the end.

There's no gloss, but it isn't bad this way either. Not bad at all.

That's the face of a future star. Everybody will realize. When they see her. Now no–one understands and doesn't want to understand. But when they stop using reasons, predictions for the future, knowledge and beliefs, once they open their eyes and see her in all her beauty, everybody will come to realize. They will be left breathless and will realize.

Alena stands up and wraps a silk light blue scarf around her head, its ends falling and touching her naked back and shoulders. Alena takes off her short pants, the only piece of clothing she has on. She stays naked. Alone and naked, before the glass door of her sister's wardrobe. She tucks her circumcised penis between her legs, joining them by softly rubbing her thighs one against the other.

Alena is excited. She spins around. She looks at her bottom, her arms, her pubic hair. In the reflection she sees herself, a beauty. She comes close to the glass, kissing it. She kisses her reflection in the mouth and rubs her breasts against its coldness. She loves herself. She leaves a lipstick mark.

Then she fumbles in the clothes and finds a bra which she stuffs with socks, as well as lace panties.

The smell of something burning comes through the window. Hay burns in the neighborhood. A small black strap dress her sister wore at the junior prom falls all over the soft skin. The small white high–heeled shoes pinch, but this is the price worth paying. A white thin jumper which is tied at the waist goes across it all.

A window is broken. Alena drags a chair in front of the wardrobe. She sits down. She pulls her dress across her knees. She crosses her legs. She feels a warm wind on her skin. With her right hand she touches the inside of her thighs. The left forefinger ends up in her mouth, playing with her tongue. Triumphant cries of primitive joy are heard.

Alena enjoys herself. She's never seen anything as attractive.

There's a merciless bang on her door.

Alena closes her eyes, throws her head back and pushes her pelvis forward. She smiles with pleasure.

A strict male voice shouts: *Open it!*

Alena begins to hug herself, imitating a love couple in a trance.

Someone breaks in and runs into the house. There aren't many of them, perhaps only one.

Alena stands up abruptly and hides in the wardrobe. There, in the dark, she feels something soft, something plush. Alena tries to stay quiet, not to utter a word, but there are some people there. There's fear. Alena begins to cry. Alena put the soft, plush thing into her mouth and bites it so as not to start sobbing.

Steps in the room. Weapons being put down. A shout.

– Is there anybody here?!

The people have returned. Fear has returned. There's no freedom.

Alena opens the wardrobe slowly and emerges shyly with a small plush lemur in her hand. Before her, she can see a young man in disheveled military uniform, with a three-day beard and a rifle in his hand. Their eyes meet. Her make-up is partly smeared with tears. After a few seconds, he asks her:
- *Girl, what's your name?*
- *Alena.*
- *Be good and tell me if there are any men in this house?*
Alena shakes her head.

LEMUR THE THIRTEENTH
GENEVA
(MONICA, 12 YEARS OLD)

Call of duty. Opening speech.

Comrades, this day will be the proudest day in your lives. (explosions, panic, flashes) *You will fight the fascist occupier with all your might. For every single fallen Soviet soldier, it is your duty to pay them back with at least ten of their lives. We won't have any mercy for defeatists, cowards and traitors.* (bewildered looks) *Should anyone dare to leave their fighting position, they will be executed on the spot…*

Hurraaaay!

Motto. There's a warrior in each one of us. Location Leningrad. Apocalyptic, dystopic vision of real history. This can be heard:

Sevodnja, dvadcatvrorava ijunja, četiri česa utra slučilos abjavljenije vojni. Germanski vojska napalji našu stranu![*]

The tramp of feet in heavy muddy boots which pinch the toes. MONIC 12 has in front of herself her right hand, dressed in a thick military coat and a warm glove made of hard material.

------

[*] Translation from Russian: *Today, on the twenty-fourth of June, at four o'clock in the morning, there was a military announcement. The German Army has attacked our side!*

MONIC 12 holds an old gun. She looks over the weapon and nowhere else. From the top of a half-decrepit building she observes sights of the destroyed city moaning in the bitter cold. A glance down to the left. A snowbound street, poles fallen down. Nothing. A glance down to the right. Two dead members of the Red Army. Comrades. An abandoned tank. Stairs standing empty. An explosion in the distance. Then nothing again. Nothing. Blood freezes from the picture of coldness. Frost reaches the heart. Even though it's so far away. Even though it's nowhere.

MONIC 12 considers a change of weapons. The members of the Soviet side have a reasonably good selection of rifles: the automatic PPS42 is a good enough piece. Not especially strong, but it will kill after a few shots; the Mosin–Nagant – a very powerful machine. Still, not so fast as others; the Tokarev SVT40. Like a beast, a predator, extremely precise and destructive; the Mosin–Nagant with a spyglass. The sniper rifle, its precision is almost perfect. On the other hand, one should take care to hold the air while shooting, as this can pose a problem in the given climate circumstances; the PPSh – absolutely the fastest weapon at play. This is what is required.

All of a sudden, a blast. For a split second the sky becomes red, fiery. One should get away from here, run while there's still time. But the steps are heavy, the breathing slow. Each breath is a death rattle. Smoke is all around. A shell has been fired.

MONIC 12 runs along the wooden roof boards. She jumps onto the stairs. She rushes out. The drama ceases for a moment. The sight is steady. A look through the half-demolished fence. A soldier rushes by in front. Red.

Ours. Behind him, up to two rusty water towers. Snow falls more and more intensely.

We are on the offensive. One solitary soldier with a white halo above his helmet, a halo with a Nazi Cross, hopelessly runs to and fro around the ruined hangar.

Shoot, fast, MONIC 12 tells herself. A miss. Reach him. Shoot again. That's it. He's dead. Bravo, MONIC 12! You've just killed CHICAGO 95.

But MONIC 12 is now in a wind–blown place. Anybody can shoot her here. She flees inside the nearby walls. Their shadows offer an illusion of safety. A moment in the corner of an empty room. A shy glance through the window. A big sign across the road: ŽELJEZNO-DOROŽNAJA STANCIJA*.

How long to stay in the shelter? Not play as a coward. That's for beginners. Play as a real warrior. Be a warrior. This is our city. There's no–one else to liberate it. Always be in front. Look death in the eyes. Kill. Kill the losers.

Here's one, out of nowhere. Aim. Zoom. A spurt of blood from his head. You've just killed TOKIOBOY. Ruins and more ruins. Windows and more windows. The street is a danger. The street is a vast icy steppe. It should be crossed. Snipers are all over the roofs. Be afraid of each step, each escape. But also be afraid of staying. Hiding is death. Attack is life. Attack!

MONIC 12 rushes out into the street, toward a wide field. She meets a few fellow soldiers, who join her. All together, onward, into eternity!

There's a meadow behind the stone fence. The meadow is a snow–covered desert with low scattered pine trees.

---

*   Russian for a railroad station.

Useless cannons in the distance. Members of the rival army emerge from behind the cannons, one by one. They still don't shoot. Neither of them. They employ tactics. MONIC 12 fills up her clip. The ammunition is here. Then an assault. Open fight. Destroy or be destroyed. Thumping of the drums inside the head. Noise. Millions of voices. Hurrayyy!

Rifles. Bombs. Shrieks of pain. Red sky. You've just killed JEREMY. You've just killed MUMBAI 14. You've just killed XYZ. You've just killed TERMINATOR 89. You've just killed KILLERMAN. You've just killed AUSYMF.CKER. You've just killed MONTEVIDEO 30. You've just killed SICILIANO 13.

You've just been killed by CAMEROON FIGTHER!

Death ensues. Monica is killed, she sits dead in front of her computer for a few moments.

A small messenger window followed by an irritating sound appears in a corner of the screen. CAMEROON FIGHTER requests connection. Connect. A video call from CAMEROON FIGHTER. Accept. The killer calling. Accept the video call.

A girl almost the same age as Monica smiles sadly from the central part of the screen. Behind her, there's a wall painted loud blue. Below her, there's a cheap white plastic chair. The girl is no fighter at all. The girl is a black full–lipped big–eyed angel.

CAMEROON FIGHTER: Where are you from?

YOU: Switzerland.

CAMEROON FIGHTER: You're beautiful.

YOU: You, too.

Someone knocks on the door.

A pause. Silence.

CAMEROON FIGHTER: Want to see my tits?

YOU: Hm... Yes.

CAMEROON FIGHTER unbuttons her white shirt. Two wounds appear in the central part of the screen instead of fresh breasts. There's an indication of bulges, but instead of nipples there are two large scabs. Still, all around them looks like the Dead Sea.

YOU: They're nice.

CAMEROON FIGHTER: No. They're gross.

YOU: What happened to them?

CAMEROON FIGHTER: They've been pressed. My mum pressed them with a hot stone so boys cannot touch me, so I don't attract them, so I don't get pregnant too soon. She says she cannot look after another child. They're gross. Gross. They look like death. I hate them.

YOU: Don't hate them.

CAMEROON FIGHTER: Show me yours.

YOU: OK.

Monica takes off her undershirt. She throws out her chest. Her breasts are small, white and firm.

CAMEROON FIGHTER: Touch them.

Monica lifts her arm and touches her left nipple.

CAMEROON FIGHTER: Both.

Monica touches the other tit, too. She fills her hands with her breasts. She closes her eyes. She sighs. She bites her lip.

CAMEROON FIGHTER: I want to be there, with you.

Monica lifts her hips. Monica caresses her neck, touches her half–open mouth. She licks them all over. Monica feels moist inside. Monica leaks.

CAMEROON FIGHTER: I want to kiss them. I hate you for being so beautiful.

Monica's eyes are closed. Monica leaks.

Someone knocks on the door. And then opens it slightly.

Her father, with a small toy, a lemur, in his hand.

– Monica, come on, please get out. You never leave this room. You eat nothing. I don't know what to do. Whenever I open the door, you sit at your computer, only in those panties which you never change. What are you doing, for god's sake? I remember, at this time two years ago, you never parted from this doll of yours, you took it everywhere, nor from your rollerblades, your ball. You went everywhere, spent time outdoors, but now... You're always alone.

– Dad, get out! You scared me. Why are you bursting into my room like that? What do you want? Get away. I hate you. Get out. Get out!

– Come to lunch. Be good, turn that off and come to the dining room.

– I'll eat here.

– Can I play with you?

– Get out.

– You're always alone.

LEMUR THE FOURTEENTH HOME FOR ABANDONED AND DISABLED CHILDREN – VALEA SCREZII, ROMANIA (DANIELA, 13 YEARS OLD)

In between fleshy breasts, pressed by a small–size bra is a big–eyed toy – a lemur.

There on ce lived an ememeemperor whose naaaame was Trojan this emperor haaaad go at's ears, and he used to call in bar bar bar ber after bar ber to shave him but whooo ever went in neeeever c c came out again for while the baaarber was shaving ing him the emperorrrr would ask what he o o o observed uncommon in him and when the bar r r ber would answer that he observed his go at's ears ears ears the emperor would immediately ly ly cuttt him into pieeeeces...[*]

---

[*] *The Emperor Trojan's Goat's Ears* is a Balkan legend about an emperor with goat's ears. Trojan is the cruelest and the most powerful emperor under the heavens. Due to his estrangement, the emperor has goat's ears, and any barber who shaved him and said afterward that the emperor had goat's ears was killed, until the appearance of a barber who told this truth to a hole dug in the earth. An elder tree grew out of the earth and children used it to make pipes. Instead of music, they let out a voice saying: The Emperor Trojan has goat's ears! The truth could not be hidden.

If she were more attentive, nurse Andiana could hear a distant muffled voice coming simultaneously from nowhere and everywhere, she could hear the earth telling a story. But she doesn't hear. She searches for Daniela, one of the center's icons. Daniela is a thirteen–year-old girl who disappears from the home every week, but always returns by herself before lunch. She regularly comes with a bleeding nose and chin. As soon as old scabs crust over, she rips them open again. They used to tie her, but since the European Health Commission's visit, this practice has been avoided whenever possible. She isn't here today, and it's slowly getting dark.

... at last it came to the turrrn of a certain bar bar bar ber who feigned illnesssss and sent his apprentice instead when the appreeeentice appeared befoooore the emperor he was as as asked why his master did nnnnot come and he answered because he is is is ill...

Daniela has been in the home since she was six years old. She's never learned to speak, and her only communication is being able to ask for lunch. She opens her mouth all the time and everywhere, she eats everything. Doctors claim that Daniela's mental development ceased at the age of four, and according to the data of the Center for Social Work, her mother threw her into the Danube at the age of three or four, somewhere near Golubac, Serbia. No–one knows how she swam across the river, it is only known that a bag with her mother's letter was found with her, a letter on wet paper, barely legible, a thin booklet and a plush toy – a lemur with blinking eyes. Daniela had spent a few weeks with animals in the Romanian border area before she was found by a fisherman. Daniela's survival was a miracle.

Unlike others, socialization isn't imposed upon her in the home. When the nurses pushed her for the first time, with the doctors' permission, between two walls of children formed while playing red rover, Daniela charged so hard into one of them, jumping with all her weight on a feeble seven–year–old boy, bit off part of his ear and carried on eating his cheek. That was the moment when they started to treat her as an animal.

... when the appreeeentice came home his master asasasasked him how he got on at the emperrrror's and the youth answered allwell and the emperor has told me that I ammmm to shave him in future then he sh sh showed the twelve duccccats he haaad received but as to the emperor's goat's earssss of that he saidddd nothingggg...

Although Daniela (who was named after a then–popular series in Romania) committed no other aggressive incident after this one, the staff have never let her approach other children in any situation that could be disturbing for her. She is kept aside, from company, from therapy, from attempts at education.

... from this tiiiime forth the appreeeentice went regularly to troooojannnn to shaaaave him and for each shaaaving he received twelveee ducatttts but he toldddd noooo one that the em em em emperor had goat's earssss at las tttt it began to w w orrrrry and torment him that he dare tell noooo one his secret the apprentice chose the last course went into the ffffield ooooutside the city, dug a h ole intooo whichhh he thrust his head annnd called out three timessss the emperor trojjjjan has goat's earssss then he filled up pppp pppp the holllle again and with his mi mi mi mind quite relieved went home...

An informal division into four groups prevails in the home. The first consists of children not worth any trouble – those incapable of learning anything, the basic rules of nutrition, hygiene and communication, or the language, or those whose physical disability prevents any perspective. The second group includes children who accidentally happen to be here – because they are without parents, because their relatives have left them here, saying the child is crazy, but in fact the only alternative for the orphan, who would be a burden for their relatives through no fault of their own, would be murder, only it's the wrong epoch for this act. This sort of protégé often lacks no intelligence, so they could be taught something and they might leave the home one day. The third kind is eternal residents – grown-ups in their twenties and thirties, whose robust hirsute bodies are imprisoned in the minds of five-year-olds. The stupid administration of the state social system – because, surprising as it may seem, the home in the vicinity of the village of Valea Screzii is a social, not a health institution, an orphanage, not a hospital – has long neglected its duties, which has made it possible for these forgotten beings to become Eternal. The fourth group is a closed infirmary for children affected with AIDS. It's a special building enclosed by a tall wall, from which no-one is ever heard. It's a forbidden town, whose chimneys sometimes let out a little white smoke. As if there were no life there.

After seven years spent on this magic hill, Daniela belongs to the cross-section of the first and third groups of protégés.

... when n n some time had passed by there sprang an eeeelder tree out of this very hole and three slender sterns grew ew ew up beautiful and straight as tapers some shepherds found this elder cut t t off one of the steeems

and maddde a pipe oooof it but as sooooon as they began to bloooow into the new pipe out bursttt the words the emperor em em emperor trojan has goat's ears the news of this strange occurrence spread immediately throooough the whole cicicicity and at last the emperor trrrrojan himself heardddd the children blowing on a pipe: the emperor trrrroj oj oj an has goat's ears ears ears he sent instantlyyyy for the bar bar bar barber's apprentice and shouted to him...

Nurse Andiana has worked here for ten years. She might as well have been a hairdresser in Bucharest, but it isn't bad this way either. A small, but certain salary. Short working hours. Transport. Free food. Andiana is thirty–five years old and she probably won't get married, as she hasn't so far. And maybe it's better this way. Her sister regularly gets beaten by her husband. If he did that to Andiana, that would be the end of him. Andiana gets off the regular path in the woods. There's less and less light, and she doesn't wish to have another lost inpatient. She knows very well she won't be fired, as it isn't easy to find heroines who would do this subhuman job for a pittance, regardless of the unemployment rate, but the stoical endurance of the head nurse's passive aggression isn't something to make her already horrible day nicer. Suddenly she seems to hear something, a voice. Wheezing and grumbling thirty meters away from her.

... heh wwwwhat is this you have been telling the people about me ttthe poor youth began at once to explain that he had indeed noticed the emperor's earsssss but had nenene ver told old old a soul of it the emperor tore his saber out of its sheath to hew the apprentice down at which the youth was so frightened that he told the whole story in its order how he had confessed himself to the earth how an elder tree had

*sprang up on the very ry ry spottt and how when a pi pi pi
pe was made of one of its sterns the taaaale was sounded in
every dirrrrection...*

Aha, there's something. In all this darkness, only a white bottom in panties that used to be white as well seethes behind the bush. That's her, Daniela. Kneeling down on the ground, she holds an open booklet in front of her eyes as if reading from it, but in fact she knows it by heart. A boy sitting by her side listens to her, watching her speechlessly. Based on the boy's uniformed gray clothes and his hairless head, Andiana realizes it's one of the AIDS boys. Andiana makes an incautious move.

Daniela spots her, takes out her toy, the lemur, and throws it into the little AIDS boy's lap. Then she grabs the book, buries her head into the grass and starts crawling on her knees, still whispering the story, no longer to the boy now, but to the wet earth. She talks to the mud, the mud on her lips, the mud in her mouth.

– *Dani, come with me, be good. Will you?*

Andiana doesn't understand the runaway girl who indifferently goes on uttering incomprehensible syllables of an incomprehensible language. She approaches her. She pulls her hair.

– *Mole! Pig! I'll put a muzzle on that crazy gob of yours!*

Daniela speaks rapidly, trying to hold her ground and raising her voice:

*...thentheemperortooktheapprenticewithhiminacarriag-
etotheplacetoconvincehimselfofthetruthofthestoryandwhen-
theyarrivedtheretheyfoundtherewasonlyasinglestemleftthe-
emperortrojanorderedapipetobemadeoutofthisstemthath-
emighthearhowitsoundedassoonasthepipewasreadyanddo-
neofthemblewintoitoutpouredthewordstheemperortrojanh-*

asgoat'searsthentheemperorwasconvincedthatnothingonth isearthcouldbehiddensparedthebarberapprenticeslifeand- henceforthallowedanybarberwithoutexceptiontocomeand- shavehim...

Even though she's grown quite strong by now, Daniela still cannot resist the experienced and skilled nurse's strong hands. Andiana holds her up, looks her in the eyes and pulls her along, back to the home. Andiana notices the booklet in Daniela's hand.

– What do you need this book for? Why the fuck do you need it! Give it to me!

Feeling like endangered prey, Daniela clenches her hand as much as possible. An unequal fight lasts for a mere ten seconds, after which only a piece of an illustrated page stays between the small thick fingers, and the rest of the book is thrown by Andiana into the woods in the heat of the moment.

It starts to rain. Daniela hugs herself, pressing her breasts, but the lemur is gone. Then, drawing from herself the last atoms of strength, she manages to break away and run back toward the boy and the thrown book. Andiana catches up with her after about thirty steps, jumps on her, slaps her in the face, hits her once, twice, with her fist, on the back, on the head.

– I'm fed up with you! I'm fed up with you all! What are you doing with my life? Stench. Sickness. Death. Madness. Death.

She gets hold of a stone and hits her on the nose, on the forehead, on the neck. The eyes. Relentlessly. She stops.

Daniela doesn't breathe. Andiana covers her with pebbles, mud, moss, bark. She makes a mound. No–one will search for Daniela. They will all be relieved. Andiana will manage to sell a story about a girl who simply got lost in the woods, never to come back.

Wet and muddy all over, Andiana returns to the administrative building. If she were more attentive, she could hear the earth breathing, mumbling, saying:

... illustrated fairy tales for children prepared by bbbogoljub savić cip cataloging in publication the national library of serbia belgrade eight two one one six three four one three six first edition savić print a hundred and eighty pages twenty–one cm print run a thousand isbn nine eight seven eight six eight six two two two three five one two cobiss rid one five five five three four eight two two.

LEMUR THE FIFTEENTH
ANDALUSIA
(CARMITA, 14 YEARS OLD)

A thin plastic thread. A needle on the lighter's fire. A pack of paper towels.

Three red roses.

The Earth on four elephants.

A winged child born in Andalusia.

Ten thousand babies smuggled into America in hollowed–out watermelons.

Lady D with burning eyes like the leader of a satanic cult.

Torn sheets of a sensationalist occult magazine in the corner of a ruin beside dried excrement. Traces of body waste also embellish the pages that, who knows when, came in handy for someone's wiping.

This ruin is visited only by those who need to relieve themselves.

Boys' mutated voices are fresh in her memory: *Gitana! Gitana!**

From somewhere, from an empty open roadside bar, a song is heard on the radio, sadness is heard on the radio:

---

*   The Spanish word for a Romani girl or woman.

Cuando no te conocía
mi vida era diferente
cuando no te conocía
vivo a espaldas de la gente...[*]

Then a rustling sound, the change of station. Another song:

Pedimietno Gitano...[**]

Pain in the memory. Pain in the stomach, concrete pain. Physical pain. While it was happening, she thought she'd cry. She thought she'd have a headache. She thought she'd feel guilty. But then it was all over. The pain was so clear, so specific. It hurts her down there. She also bleeds a little. She wipes the blood with a handkerchief. She waits for three roses to appear. No. It's one rose, one big rose which slowly covers the entire surface of the lace–edged white silk.

It was so hot there. Plaster had fallen off the walls. Bricks. Grass peeks out from between the bricks at some places. There's neither a roof nor a window. Instead of them, holes, high holes. A half–demolished house on the way to nowhere, to Carmita's home.

As she was being stripped off, she thought at one point that it was embarrassing she hadn't shaved her legs. She'd never done this before, but she meant to, that day, that Friday, to dare, to try. Then she remembers smiling

---

[*] Translation from Spanish: Until I met you, my life was different, until I met you, I hide from other people…

[**] A traditional Spanish Romani engagement party.

to herself, silently, attempting to breathe as calmly as possible. Then from these thoughts she went back to the trauma of this ruin, among this silly powerful little heap of stone limbs and rough, clumsy movements, among the young with already old mean faces, among these people, yes, they are people, if boys, who keep her mouth shut with their dirty hands and push into her, nudging, smiling, hating each other. Those who are pushed aside look on, masturbating. They come all over her, shrieking. One of them is singled out as a leader and stays on her the longest. He squeezes her breasts. A painful face. More painful than hers, indifferent.

And the silk handkerchief had been given to her by her mother, exactly on Carmita's twelfth birthday, when she talked to her for the first time as to a person, as to a serious being. She told her:

I give you this, as my mother gave me once. It's a female thing. After your proposal, but before your betrothal, the groom's female relatives will take you into one room. Then they'll strip you off and spread your legs, like this. Like this, exactly. And the oldest one will touch you here with two fingers to see if you're a virgin. Are you a virgin? Carmita, understand what this means? You're no longer young enough not to understand.

Mother touched her down there. She stuck her finger and circled with it on the surface. It felt pleasant.

Yes. You certainly are. You're a virgin. Mother takes care of you. Then grandma will let a drop of your blood, but don't worry, it doesn't hurt at all and, if you're a virgin, a small trace will remain on the handkerchief which looks like three roses. The three roses will dry out, and the handkerchief will stay as a pledge in the decades to come, as a proof that I've taken care of you. Only then can you get married, Carmita. If there are no three roses, there's no marriage. That's why you'd better take care. I have to tell you while there's still time.

This is what her mother told her, and then Carmita pictured this event in her mind during the night. The whole *pedimiento* ceremony.

The groom is entirely abstract, but he still has an appearance. He looks, more or less, like David DeMaria, only a little younger. Everybody looks at them, but he cares only for her. He tells her something quietly, to her ear, touching her hair. What he says isn't important. He's got a beautiful voice which speaks so quietly, when he talks about what only the two of them know, when he reveals a secret about some of the present guests. The two of them laugh at that secret, trying not to let anyone notice the laugh. Now they have something in common.

She imagines her *pedimiento*, passing the thin plastic thread through the needle she burned on the lighter's flame until a moment ago. The needle is clean. The thread is thin. Her thumb and forefinger are used for catching. Her left thumb and forefinger get hold of her labia and pull them out, outside the body cavity. Her right thumb and forefinger hold the needle tight, pressed against the skin. She breathes through her nose. Fast, unbearably irregularly.

She'll come to the place where it happened. She'll stitch herself up, she's decided, she'll stitch herself up, with no grinding of her teeth at all, with no voice let out, the same way she was ripped apart. She'll move everything back to its place. Everything will be all right. Three roses will adorn the white fabric.

She should have gone straight home, but the body did its part. She had to hide among the walls where many had hidden in order to relieve themselves. She'd dropped by at this ruin lots of times, for years. But then. Sweat. Sweat and pain.

But then.

Pedimiento Gitano...

And she came to this place again. To turn back time. To re–pack things.

She prepares for pain in advance. To behave like it already hurts, and then, when it actually begins to hurt, she won't even notice the unpleasantness. She shivers. She stabs her flesh like a coat with a missing button.

The tactic works to a certain extent. The difference between a painless state and a painful state isn't as big as Carmita expected. Suddenly she pierces both labia. The first step back, toward regained carelessness, is taken, two more stitches on the left and three on the right. She thought that six stitches would be enough. There were also six of them, the boys. Six insane cocks.

She already knows which premises she'll choose. A reception room on the way to town. She's been there once, at Rosa and Rafael's wedding. It was so beautiful, as in a fairy tale. They drove in a Mercedes. Rosa had a crown. She was the most beautiful woman in the world.

From left to right, with all her might. Heat and sticky sweat. Flies on turds. Flies on her thighs, on her nose. On her fingers.

She wouldn't get out alone, they would open the car door for her. She would wait for a while. She would let the guests fret for a few seconds before they see her in all her beauty. Then she would stretch out her freshly shaven leg, putting her white leather high–heeled sequin sandal on the sidewalk first and only then would she appear before everyone, elegant, clutching at her lavish wedding dress. They would all start clapping.

From right, hard again, through both labia. Blood, blood gushes down the body canyon toward the anus. The sensation of the thread passing through a tight door, through a narrow passage, along the votary's road, through a thin hole in the flesh. This squeaking sound. Unbearable music.

What about music? She would enter the hall, and there she would be met by DeMaria personally. This would be a surprise that he, the fiancé, had prepared for her. David would take her by the hand and lead her onto the small stage, before all the delighted eyes. Then she would wink at her and begin singing *Que yo no quiero problemas...* In between the lines, he would whisper to her: *Be my Chenoa, sing along with me.* She would sing, sing more beautifully than ever before, at the top of her voice. *...perdona lo que dije, y no quise decir***. At the top of her voice.

She shrieks at the top of her voice at the fourth jab. With time, it doesn't get easier, quite the opposite. There's more and more blood. The paper towels on which she sits are already totally soaked. A lizard scurries by on its way to a hole in the wall. Birds chirp. Nothing that happens to humans seems to be of any concern to them. A cricket. Heat.

---

* Translation from Spanish: As I don't want any problems...

** Translation from Spanish: ... forgive me what I told you, I didn't mean to.

Everybody will be dancing, all evening long. Everybody will be welcome. The rich, as well as those who live on the streets and pick stuff from dumpsters. Everybody will be clapping and greeting her: *Carmita! Carmita!* The celebration will last long into the night. They will all be kissing her. Mum, dad, brother, sisters, aunts, everybody, everybody – their smiling faces will flash before her eyes and congratulate her on the successfully outlined three roses. They will be kissing her.

She already trembles now. From fear, from hope, from physical weakness. She can barely keep her eyes open from pain. Everything stings her. She can hardly clasp her labia once more. She holds her breath and doesn't breathe, in order to press the needle onto the right place for the fifth time. With the last atoms of will she forces the sharp steel into herself, into her cunt, into her life. Only one stitch to go. Only one.

She will get plenty of gifts. A plasma TV and a vacation at the seaside.

They will all be kissing her.

They will all be congratulating her.

She can no longer open her eyes. One stitch to go. The pain is so strong. She has no strength.

Her head falls. She feels she is going to faint. She mustn't let this happen. She cannot open her eyes. A lizard scurries by on its way to the hole. The windows are high above. *Cuando no te conocía.*

Carmita sits in the ruin with neither a roof nor a window, leaned against a wall, with her bleeding legs spread apart.

The Earth is placed on the back of four elephants.

A winged child is born.

Three roses on white silk.

A small plush lemur thrown into the dust long ago, pissed all over.

LEMUR THE SIXTEENTH
BUDAPEST – LAKITELEK
(ANIKA, 11 YEARS OLD)

This is your last chance. So be good, Anika. Mind what you do this time.

The jury consists of gigantic heroes arranged in a circle. Petrified, they watch her reproachfully. She's condemned. She wants to approach them. Between them and her is a too–wide plateau of stone and concrete, gigantic, made not for people, but for subjects of empires, kingdoms, nations, republics.

Above all, the judge. Archangel Gabriel. Half–spread wings. Boasting. Putting on airs. Raising a golden wreath. The gold starts to burn. He'll put it on her head. He appears to be mild, but he isn't. She feels his blessed warmth.

They have all come down on her. Angels and heroes alike. They send their breath of smog to her. They'll kill her this way. They'll poison her. She rolls up the back car window at the last moment and saves herself from her fate. The judgment thumps on the glass from the outside. Exile.

The world rewinds.

The streets have curbs. Streets are an enclosed space for movement. People wear gray suits, knee–length skirts, leather shoes, stockings, faces. Human faces are animal faces. Feelings do not exist. People invent feelings in order not to think about the fact that they are animals. But they are. Here are animal faces on human heads, passing by. Backward. Missus weasel, dog–boy, mister dolphin, owl–girl, elephant, marmot, jay, rat, monkey...

Overpasses move toward Anika. They accept her underneath, among their legs. They swallow her. She's no longer.

Don't worry at all. You'll see how good life is there. Lakitelek is a place out of a fairy tale. Lakes, friendly people. Wonderful. If anyone could have afforded anything like that to me... But you, today's children. Ungrateful of you.

Budapest goes away. It leaves the Škoda Octavia on the highway, it also leaves Anika, who is inside. Buildings disappear in the distance. Lampposts leave. The wires joining them are intertwined. They somehow fall. They are suspended. They grow in depth under the burden of all lives being led below them. Any life is dreadful. Anika knows this. She doesn't know exactly what to say about it, nor to whom, but she knows. She knows that happiness doesn't consist of flowers, as she is made to believe. She knows that love isn't happiness, as she is made to believe. She knows that land isn't happiness, as she is made to believe. She knows that happiness doesn't consist of children, as she is made to believe.

The power cables are on fire. The Škoda Octavia rushes along the highway around which two lines of flame stretch. The asphalt melts from their heat. This is happiness. This is something closest to happiness, for Anika.

Anika rolls down the window. She watches the outside world. Anika is cold. Anika rolls up the window. She no longer watches the outside world, but the window. The outside world unfolds on the two-dimensional glass surface. The main roles are taken over by tiny, nondescript houses, industrial facilities, then clouds. At last, the sun.

As soon as it's started, the film gets interrupted by a powerful sound effect – a strong blow to the windscreen. It's a sparrow. A sparrow hit the glass with full force. The glass didn't crack, but a slight blood stain remained after this feeble creature. The creature is feeble. Small. The creature is past. A sparrow. A mini-sparrow. A mini-book. Mini-dad. A clever girl. A mini-girl. A mini-beauty. A mini-memory. A mini-truth. A mini-fire. A mini-hatred. A mini-anguish. A mini-death.

Anika is sorry for the sparrow. Anika is cold. She warms herself by imagined fires. She is roused by the voice of the bulky social worker from the passenger seat.

They said you were all right. They said you had potential, you weren't among those not worth bothering about. Psychologists. We have to trust them. Still, some things... When you were last in a foster family, you couldn't restrain yourself. You burned their entire roof. And they were good people. Mr. Gyula may have slapped you in the face once, but so what? He has two jobs, and you aren't that easy to live with. You're heavy, Anika, heavy as lead. And Mr. Gyula has two jobs. He gets home, and you make trouble. And that happened only once. You have to endure. You cannot choose how to live. You don't have such a privilege. And, what did you achieve by doing so? The people lost their roof, and you returned to the home. And was it any better at the home? Didn't they beat you there? You have to think a bit, Anika. Be wise!

Anika doesn't listen. She shivers from some coldness. She hugs herself so as to be warmer. It doesn't help. The Škoda Octavia is overtaken by an ambulance with rotating lights on, and then it pulls up five hundred meters in front of Anika. There's a white car there, completely destroyed after crashing into the road verge. A middle-aged woman lies there and a pool of thick black and red liquid spreads under her head, with placid certainty. That's blood mixed with oil. One spark would be enough to make this disconcerting sight worthwhile, to make non–life a life. To make Anika warm. And from in front, a banal shift of gaze.

I cannot look at this. Terrible. TERRIBLE! Anika, don't you look either. How can you?

Social workers, psychologists, teachers, nurses, all that system above her, foster parents, bullies, other kids, people, all that country couldn't touch a chord with Anika. She is seized upon from all sides, tied up, stolen her time, talked to, preached at, understood, taken, given, at any moment and any place they want something from her. Anika doesn't understand what. Anika simply looks coolly and warms her look on the sights of misery. Why? Who knows? She doesn't. And if she doesn't know why, neither will those figures who steal her from herself of their own accord, who never leave her alone. The river is black and it flows in the opposite direction to Anika. A flock of turtledoves chases her with no success. Oak and linden trees hitchhike, hoping they won't be picked up. Houses implode under the pressure of those living inside them. Overpasses threaten to collapse in on those passing underneath. Everything begins to glow. Those flying turtledoves, as well. They turn into bullets.

Anika dips her hand into her panties, feeling for a tiny cardboard box. She opens it with her forefinger, thumb and middle finger, and then she pats the matches inside. Anika is tranquil. Everything is all right.

A restless voice is heard from the front seat again:

If you burn something here, too, even a blade of grass, you're in for living at the home until you're eighteen. And you know what it's like at the home. You know very well. So, mind what you do, Anika. Be good and listen to the Tots.

A fly seeks its happiness inside the car. It flies tirelessly from left to right and back again, right above Anika's head. Anika follows it with her eyes. Anika is on the watch. At one moment she abruptly lifts her arms and, like a predator, she claps her hands along the fly's expected line of movement. Then she spreads her hands. The white substance of the black insect's body has filled out part of the canyon of the life line. One small leg still twitched.

A sparrow bumped into the windshield. A small spot of its blood dried on the glass.

A woman lay on the highway asphalt.

The remains of the fly were on her skin.

Everything is black.

Everything is red.

Anika sows death.

Come on. We've arrived. You see how beautiful the yard is. You can play to your heart's content. But knowing you, you'd better not play. Come now. Be good and mind what you do.

Anika is good.

Anika gets out of the car. The first thing she spots is a hay storage barn behind the house.

Her new foster parents greet her and kiss her. Mr. Tot gives her a bar of stuffed chocolate and a second–hand plush toy – a long–lashed female lemur.

He tells Anika:

We'll have a great time together, won't we? We love kids very much.

Anika sows death.

LEMUR THE SEVENTEENTH
URFA SUBURBS – TURKEY
(AIDA, 9 YEARS OLD)

A rectangle which Aida holds on to as if to her last hope.
This paper is just big enough for Aida to curl up on it and
feel like she's on her own island.
This paper is just big enough for Aida to imagine she were
on a raft floating on a rough ocean.
Aida is all alone in the world, after a shipwreck. She's the
only survivor. The others are dead. Thoroughly, definitely
dead. Aida is alone. The raft. The waves. Alone.
Some messages from an ancient people or god himself
are left on this vessel which luckily came her way, like a
godsend, exactly when she was losing her breath. How
important this is! How exciting!
These signs must address only her, since she is left alone.
And god knows who he leaves alive, who he leaves
messages for. A message for the last person in the world.
It should be deciphered.
What do these signs convey to her?
A fork. A rake. A trident used for catching dangerous fish.
A black background, a white sign. Or a white background,
a black sign? E.
What kind of a sign is that?
The sign seems to go through a gate. It reminds of a tool,

a screwdriver, a wrench. Something is supposed to be fixed, opened. In life. A shape almost square. Or it's a house, seen from above. A house without doors, but a house with two rooms, upstairs and downstairs. Left or right. Who lives in that house?

Is that the house in which Aida will live when she grows up?

Then beneath, the same sign again. F.

Someone broke one tooth. The fish escaped. Or the catch simply looked like fish, but was in fact a rock against which one horn broke.

The same sign as the previous one. Only one part is missing, as if the repair was badly done, so instead of getting better, things got worse, lacking a part. Something is missing. One wall of the house is demolished. Someone wants to get inside, but he is too big, so he cannot pass through the entrance. Or someone wishes her evil. Simply, someone is evil and demolishes her house, starting from one corner.

Next. A blunt hammer. A chipped flag. A tin advertising sign rotating in the wind. P.

She is afraid of the demolisher, the invader, the villain breaking into her house, and out of fear she hides herself in the room, upstairs. She locks herself in. Finally she has a room of her own. She is safe there, but it is a matter of time before the bully knocks on her door, too. If he demolished the wall, he won't even notice the door.

The next sign. Corners. Spread hands. A pole. T.

Wait a minute. She isn't made of glass, after all. She herself can fight back. Little though she may be, she's learned how to deal with people, wandering about the streets. Stand up. Fly into a passion. She knows, there are a lot of lunatics, but how can others know if she is even crazier, ready for who knows what. This sign shows her, upright, with outstretched arms, ready for an encounter with any monster. She is going to fight. Till death!

Then. The sun. The full moon. A head. A wheel. A ring. O. She just acts before herself. She realizes again how slight and weak she is, how anyone can crush her. Strive as she might, an adult's single serious look will turn her into a mere baby, a fragile, sickly creature prone to fear. This is why she'll lock herself in. She'll build walls all around, everywhere, in a circle.

Then that strange pattern. A joke. A mistake. A children's toy. Z.

Then she will curl up in that circle of fear, huddle into herself. She'll bow her head down to her bent knees. She won't look into the danger. She'll look into herself. Then everything might be over. Just like that. Aida will stay alone. In herself.

A corner. A broken line. A broken stick. L.

She finds the hiding pleasing, but it's forbidden. As usual, she never knows in advance what is forbidden, and what isn't. She gets to know this only after she's punished. Now she's also punished for her fear, for her stupidity and lack of information. Now she imagines the demolisher from the beginning. A man, tall, grown–up, with no face, with all faces of the world. Now he's there, in front of her. He sends her into the corner. Now only the corner exists for her. What happens behind her back is beyond her comprehension. It doesn't even exist.

Again. P.

Anew, there in the corner, she locks herself in. As in the

room, again, but she knows there's no longer the room. She locks herself inside herself.

E.

Let's start all over. A house again. Or it's just that she daydreams about the room, the house, rewinding her mind. She imagines, and she's still in the corner all the while. From the beginning.

D.

Rewinding her mind, she attempts once again to make a circle around her, to shut herself in. But a familiar force stops her halfway. Aida only makes a semicircle.

P.

A new attempt to shut herself in the room.

E.

A house again.

C.

And once again she tries to get cocooned, to shut herself in, to draw a circle around her soul. She almost succeeds, but the adult force is still there to interrupt her before the work's done.

F.

A demolished house.

D.

Half–escape into half–self.

E.

A house of open doors.

D.

Half–escape.

F.

A house demolished.

C.

Get cocooned.

Z.

Curl up. Look into oneself.

P.

Run away. Attempt. For the last time.

A demolished house. A house. A corner. A circle. A room. A semicircle. Smaller and smaller signs. Try as she may to decipher them, Aida doesn't comprehend where they lead her. Where's the way to the land.

Aida drifts on this paper across the ocean of medical waste on an illegal dump near Urfa. Aida collects unbroken jars, measuring cylinders, syringes whose color is preserved, everything that appears to be unused or still usable. Aida slips all this into her sack, then takes it to the collection center where, together with other children, she washes these objects, repacks them with clean paper and sells at the flea market.

Now she's already two hours late with her delivery. Instead of working, she half–consciously gapes at a white piece of paper decorated with different–size letters on which she sits.

– *Where are you, you little piece of shit? Am I supposed to wait for you? I'll kill you now. Oh my, you'll be good. Otherwise, you're fucking dead!*

Between her boss's voice and the strong blow to her ear with his spread palm which necessarily follows, perhaps about twenty seconds will pass, judging from the distance of the voice. Aida suddenly comes back from the ocean to the dump and hysterically begins to forage under her paper raft. She can only feel broken plastic, cotton wool and glass. Nothing of any use. She also touches a plush thing deep beneath the layers of discarded stuff. She pulls it out – a plush monkey.

That's him, her god – he came from the land and he'll take her to a sand beach with palms on which he lives. At the last moment, in front of a huge wave. He sent her all those messages. He'll explain them to her in detail. He'll tell her stories. The two of them will be together, alone in the world.

As she anticipated, a rough palm falls down on her small right ear, which is slightly lopsided. The other palm finds its way to the other ear. It hurts like it was hit with as much force as possible, but Aida knows that only a third of the boss's energy was used and that strong blows are still to come.

As fists land all over her head and back, Aida imagines being in her house, in her room, locked in, cocooned inside herself. Punished. In the corner.

There's only a corner. What happens behind her back is beyond her comprehension. It doesn't exist at all.

E

F P

T O Z

L P E D

P E C F D

E D F C Z P

____

F E L O P Z D

D E F P O T E C

LEMUR THE EIGHTEENTH
BOUARFA, MOROCCO
(JASMIN, 13 YEARS OLD)

Infirmary for organic non–matter.

Half past six.

You can hear tin banging against tin.

You know it's a plate falling on a metal cupboard.

You lift your heavy lids.

You can see a female face.

The female face bends over you.

A female hand sticks a spoonful of rice porridge into your mouth.

Your lips spread open with great effort.

Half the porridge falls out.

Female hands remove the covers routinely.

Female hands lift your nightgown.

Female hands take off your soaked diapers.

Female hands wipe you with a wet towel, and then put on new, clean diapers. Female hands cover you.

The female face disappears.

The murmurs of the day melt into an indeterminable and with time more and more insignificant whole. Now you can hardly remember arriving here and those who accompanied you, father, brother.

And on that day when they first brought you here, you only saw a myriad of thickly arranged beds. Those beds used to be bunk beds, but they've been converted into single beds, which is visible from their poles. The poles are made of metal. There are springs in between them. A small room, subterranean, with a low ceiling. Along the edges of the walls condensed damp corrodes the mortar. Mould spreads ominously. Stale air. The air is not breathable, it's suffocating. Odors of sweat and boiled vegetables are mixed. The vegetables are onions. The kitchen is on the same level, next door.

There's nothing brought from home. You get stripped naked. Bathed. You are given new clothes. You are thrown onto a mattress.

Half past ten.

And experienced female hands turn you on one side, seemingly sloppily but skillfully.

Female hands turn you on your stomach.

Female hands spread anti-bacterial cream over your bedsores, gently, as if they were their own, as if they hurt them.

This anti-voice *sssss* produced by sucking air through teeth isn't produced by you, ever, but by the nurse who nourishes you with anti-bedsore spreads.

The sores on your back caused by the lack of movement, the lack of freedom which would touch the skin, become thicker and deeper. The flesh gapes open.

Half past twelve.

Tin against tin.

A plate falls on a metal cupboard.

A female face bends over you.

A female hand sticks a spoon into your mouth.

It's lunchtime.

Day means nothing here. Things happen routinely and you come to learn how to measure time according to them. Time means nothing here. You practice killing it. The more you sleep, the faster it will pass. But you can't sleep because it hurts, because everything is difficult. Because you have no peace. You stretch time, condense it, play with it, like a cat with a mouse. You chase it so it can pass sooner. You kill time until it kills you.

Day means nothing here. Night means everything here.

They brought you at night. When you were little, you could walk and draw and write, although you didn't want to show anyone your drawings and scribbled letters, because punishment or ridicule would follow. When you were little, you could feel strength and pain and resistance. And then weakening, part by part. Torso. Legs. Hands. Shoulders. Neck. Everything. Everything but the heart. It still resists. Then bedriddenness. Constrained attention. And, finally, that night they brought you here, to the female ward of the infirmary for patients affected by dystrophy and other bedridden patients. Father and brother. They told you: *Be good, Jasmin. We'll come tomorrow to visit you.* They haven't appeared since then, for a year and a half now. How many days is that? You don't know. Day means nothing here.

You remember the feeling, but memory loses its significance with time, as everything else. When you remember, you force yourself to sleep. You don't manage to fall asleep, but the memory fades away.

Night means everything here. Dull sounds of pain can be heard at night. Sudden shrieks. Pointless suicide attempts by suffocating. Girls and women stop breathing, willingly, with no physical obstacle whatsoever. And then, nonetheless, just when they are about to faint, their bodies cheat them yet again and inhale. Night is for dreams. Night is for calling out to your family, acquaintances, never expressed loves. Night is for inarticulate mumbling. Voices, those unbearable voices are the sign that everything is all right. That it's good.

When there are no voices, it's death.

Night is also for dying. Hearts die out. Those small, stunted, weakened muscles strive as long as they can. They beat silently, hardly visibly. Life no longer sings. Life whispers. Life falls asleep. The heart withers. Physically. There's no suffering. The body simply goes off. In silence.

When there are no voices, it's death.

Night means everything here.

Everything that happens, happens at night. Asis the keeper comes at night. He makes a round of all the beds. He turns on the light and undresses the women and girls. He takes the covers off them, then he pulls off their nightgowns. After that, he watches them naked. At times he touches them. Most often he simply goes round the beds and watches. For hours on end.

A newly arrived girl usually gets upset when she experiences this for the first time, but she gets used to it later on. At first she rolls her eyes, lets out some sounds, calls the nurses. But there's no–one here at night, in this basement, except Asis. Asis takes care of the heat, Asis keeps watch, Asis is there. Sometimes it so happens that you, uncovered, fall asleep while Asis watches you, moaning.

Night means everything here. One night he came up to you and, as usual, as many times before, he took off the sheet and the thin fabric of your nightgown. He watched you for a couple of minutes and then started to pat you on the head. He began to moan, but not as usual. This time he cried. He patted you on the head and cried. You lay naked. What else could you do? Then he put a small plush toy on your pillow, next to your head, a pink-tailed monkey. Asis's tears fell on your face. You wanted to break free. All this annoyed you. You wanted nothing from him. Nothing. His tears fell on your lips. Asis then covered you and went to the opposite bed. He uncovered another young woman and started to moan again.

Since then, I've been in your dreams talking to you. You dream of me lying on a pillow, next to your head, like a threat, saying all kinds of things. Incessantly talking.

Everybody has been silent before you, always and everywhere. They were silent when mum disappeared. They were silent when you became bed–ridden. They were silent when they brought you here. I'm the only one who talks to you.

And monkeys don't talk, Jasmin. You know that.

You know you'll wake up to find me beside you, on the pillow, keeping silent, not opening my mouth. You'll wake up, but you'll know that day means nothing here. Because night means everything here.

Night. And then:

You'll hear tin banging against tin.

You'll know it's a plate falling on a metal cupboard.

You'll lift your heavy lids.

You'll see me on the pillow.

You'll see a female face above you.

A female hand sticks a spoonful of rice porridge into your mouth.

Your lips spread open with great effort.
Half the porridge falls out.

LEMUR THE NINETEENTH
BARCELONA
(LORA, 11 YEARS OLD)

June is a month when everything starts to tilt toward south, both people and buildings collapse from fatigue caused by inaction and from unquenchable mental heat. Hector is a native Catalan, a prototype of the preconceived notion of a Mediterranean man, tall, thin and tanned. Hector is in his mid–thirties and he is slow at waking up. He wakes up not with difficulty, but slowly, because he likes to stretch himself out under the silk cover on his wide Natuzzi bed as long as rays of sunlight suffuse the room completely through slightly open blinds. The moment has come and Hector descends barefoot to the lower level of his cosy loft apartment in a building in *Ronda del Litoral*. It is pleasant, he thinks to himself, to feel your feet touch the dry decking.

Downstairs, in the white Snaidero kitchen *by Pininfarina*, he is greeted by Whisper. Whisper is an American, three years his junior, short and irresistible, with a bright, open look in her eyes which on first sight conveys an accurate impression about their owner's quality education.

Whisper and Hector live together and love each other.

WHISPER: Good morning, love.

HECTOR: Good morning, love.

WHISPER: How did you sleep? You didn't toss and turn much last night.

HECTOR: Yes, I slept well, excellently.

Whisper and Hector kiss each other, not minding the bad morning breath. Then they both turn toward the bathroom and survey the space from the bathroom door to the kitchen table. They address the place they are observing.

WHISPER: Good morning, Lora.

HECTOR: Good morning, Lora.

WHISPER: How did you sleep?

HECTOR: Yes, how did you sleep?

LORA: ...

Columbus haughtily points his forefinger, the masts, like countries humiliated in a war, silently collaborate with space, thousands of naked bodies with towels over their shoulders flock to the beach, and from the empty place which this couple is looking at no answer is heard, no voice, no sound. No gesture is seen because no-one is there. Emptiness.

HECTOR: Well, you cannot be fresh and ready for school in the morning if you watch video clips until late. How many times do we have to tell you?

WHISPER: She'll be great. A red grapefruit juice and our Lora will be as fresh as a daisy. Right?

HECTOR: Hm, juice cannot solve all problems.

WHISPER: Come on, come on. Love, how many eggs would you like?

HECTOR: Three.

WHISPER: Lora, you? How many?

LORA: ...

Whisper absent-mindedly muses on the collision of the sky and the earth in the sfumato of the horizon. Whispering the melody of a popular song, she prepares mildly boiled eggs, puts them in porcelain bowls and places them before Hector and Lora. Hector reminisces in his head on the touch of a rock covered with algae swaying on slight waves, he cuts black Norwegian bread and puts thin slices down on the table. Lumps of Camembert join the slices. Two liters of perfect temperature filtered water find themselves in the midst of this conceptual morning arrangement.

HECTOR: Eat, Lora.

WHISPER: Really, eat, Lora. You're skinny. I saw you yesterday when you were looking in the mirror. You pinched the fat on your hips, as if you had any. You're skin and bones, Lora.

HECTOR: You're at that sensitive age. Girls start to worry about their looks then, so they go on some absurd diets. Have you heard of anorexia?

WHISPER: Or when they pretend to eat, and then run to the toilet and throw up what they've eaten. That's bulimia. A disease, you understand.

HECTOR: If you feel ill at ease in your own body, feel free to tell us. We're here to help you, no one will scold you.

WHISPER: Take some, eat. Be good.

Emptiness eats emptiness, not mildly boiled eggs and cheese. This is why the food in front of Lora remains untouched. There's no-one on the chair, except a carefully placed plush pink-tailed lemur. There's no-one.

Hector is both a whole per se and part of being, he's both vanity and hope, and an independent on-line application development engineer. Whisper is the silence and noise of the world, she's prayer at each move, freedom to be beauty, to give, and a regular freelance graphic designer with the international telecommunications company Orange. They both work from home, and their work place is a balcony with two computers, with a view expanding over the world's central sea, over everything, over nothing.

HECTOR: Any homework?

LORA: ...

HECTOR: If I were you, I would sign up for Chinese lessons. I think that's important today.

WHISPER: Who knows? Perhaps the whole hysteria about the Chinese expansion is slightly premature?

HECTOR: It's not all about economy, but cultural influence as well. Look at the painters.

WHISPER: You're right, Zhang Xiaogang, Zeng Hao. You're often in the right.

HECTOR: *Xièxie.*[*]

WHISPER: Sign up, Lora. You're good at languages.

LORA: ...

WHISPER: Come. Time for school.

The entity of nothingness abandons the family dining table and advances toward the front door. Where space is, life takes root. Where life is, death takes root, non–life. Whisper and Hector follow yet again the non–life with their eyes. Hector opens the door to the emptiness. Whisper caresses it on the non–hair and kisses it on the non–forehead. The emptiness goes away and leaves nothingness behind. Standing in front

---

[*] 'Thank you' in Chinese.

of the door and looking outside, into the building hall, Hector and Whisper are having a quiet talk.

HECTOR: I'm worried about her.

WHISPER: Why?

HECTOR: You know yourself what awaits her and us, besides herself, during the painful process of growing up: puberty, boys, nights out, mistakes, drugs, unwanted pregnancy...

WHISPER: Come on, you watch way too many films. We'll be fine with her. She's a good child.

HECTOR: Good, but slightly naïve.

WHISPER: No reason to worry. Trust me.

Corridors are chronotopes of crime and love. Corridors are places of unexpected happenings, in books and films. In life, corridors are places of nothing. Hector feels himself part of the corridor for a moment. Then Hector suddenly remembers something, so he runs into the dining room and hurriedly returns, holding the lemur carelessly by the tail. Whisper remains baffled and indifferently tranquil.

HECTOR (raising the hand with the lemur): Hey, Lora. Hey!!!! Come back! You've forgotten to take the toy, your Aya!

Silence is silence because it cares nothing about voice, because it hears nothing, because it thinks nothing in any categories of sound. Silence goes never to return, into oblivion. Whisper and Hector give up and go back inside. They go out on the balcony into the coolness of a large reed sunshade.

WHISPER: You know, this game is stupid.

HECTOR: Yes, a nonsensical experiment.

WHISPER: It isn't for us, is it?

HECTOR: It isn't. Yet.

WHISPER: And that pressure to have kids. We're accountable to no–one but ourselves.

HECTOR: We don't have to do anything we don't want to.

WHISPER: Shall we go to the beach?

HECTOR: You think the time is ripe to open the season?

WHISPER: Well yes, look at the weather. Leave the work for tonight.

HECTOR: Let's go.

Whisper and Hector grab some large towels, throw them over their shoulders and go out. On his way, Hector throws the lemur into the waste basket. The water is still slightly cold, but pleasant, refreshing. The boats swaying on slight waves confirm each human thought.

All those who have been to the beach have been right.

LEMUR THE TWENTIETH
BERLIN
(SLAVICA, 7 YEARS OLD)

The festival of experimental theater and multi–media forms of artistic expression takes place at an unusual location, on the third floor of Potsdamer Platz Arkaden Shopping Center, which has been devoid of its commercial purpose for the benefit of contemporary art, specially for this occasion for a couple of days, with the generous assistance of the German Ministry of Culture and several EU funds.

Berta arrives at the H&M store for the projection of the work *Prohibited for Gypsies and Dogs*. From the information leaflet she learns it's some sort of a film. The authors found two abandoned Roma children, beggars in the streets of Skopje, Former Yugoslav Republic of Macedonia, and put small caps with barely visible little cameras on their foreheads. They also hung another two tiny cameras on a couple of stray dogs. The viewers will be able to simultaneously follow one day in the lives of the dogs and abandoned children in an interesting and interactive way, and to make comparison of those sights, so as to discern themselves which sights are the children's and which are the dogs'.

The projection actually takes place in dressing rooms and, accordingly, the viewer is always alone when watching this accomplishment. Alone and shut in. Berta closes the door and sits in the center of the cubicle where there's a round swivel chair. Before that, she takes a remote control from the chair, so she can pause and re-play each moving image.

All of a sudden, there's darkness. Berta is alone, closed in the darkness. Street sounds can be heard. Strange languages.

The projection begins on all four walls around Berta, including the inner side of the cubicle door.

Ahead. The first camera moves along a cracked sidewalk. The view slows down next to some cardboard boxes, beside open, half-empty cans and pieces of bread.

Behind. Berta turns around on the chair in order to see another projection. A great number of people pass in front of camera number two. People's legs in boots, shoes, sneakers. In a rush. It starts to rain. The camera doesn't move. A static take.

On the third wall, on the right, darkness out of which light barely emerges, from somewhere above. Then a glance up. A glance through the small holes on a slightly open manhole. The glance goes down. So it happens. Several times.

Opposite that wall, a few small naked kids hop in a puddle. Then we shift our gaze aside and run out onto the street. We stand in front of a line of cars waiting at the traffic lights, at the distance of about twenty meters.

Berta decides to stay turned to that side.

Our eyes move left and right, quickly, slightly hysterically. The cars start to move, slowly, then faster and faster. The view doesn't change. The cars come closer, to ten meters, five meters. The cars honk their horns. The cars flash their headlights. Some of them slow down. Some rush even more aggressively. At the last moment, before the view changes. Kids' laughter can be heard. You can see the smiles on the faces of the kids who point their fingers at Berta. After about half a minute, the eyes turn toward the street again. Cars stand still at the traffic lights again.

The cars start to move. The cars honk their horns. The cars flash their headlights. The cars slow down and speed up, turn. The view moves aside at the last moment. The kids laugh.

The street again. The cars. The last moment... Until exhaustion.

Berta decides it's time to shift her eyes a little. But at that moment a woman approaches the scene. We can see her slapping the face of the owner of the view, saying:

Slavica, wanna kill yourself? Wanna kill yourself? No. I'll kill you.

Slaps land below the view, which is accompanied by their sound effects. Then an adult pulls the owner of the view somewhere, across a floor, one would say. She is dragged into a half–demolished building, into a hallway. She's beaten all the while.

Berta gets uncomfortable. She no longer experiences this as a film, as a performance. She takes the remote and places a finger on the button which pauses projection 4. She doesn't stop it.

The view moves into the basement of the building. The basement floor is flooded, so the water almost reaches the ankles. There are some cages with dogs in the basement. The dogs bark, upset. Just a couple of them don't move. Are they alive? The view gets thrust into one of the cages. The dogs growl all around. The view gets locked.

You think you can fuck with me. You'll be good, just wait till you get hungry. You'll be good.

The person leaves. Small kids' hands appear before the eyes. In the hands a plush toy, bitten all over. The hands throw the toy. The hands block the view. The hands aim at a spot under the camera. The hands hit with all their might. The hands...

LEMUR THE LAST
AND THE FIRST
BELGRADE
(TANJA, 29 YEARS OLD)

It's July 2010.

Why does she do that?

She tortures the children till exhaustion.

She leads them beyond the limits of endurance.

She teaches them helplessness.

She enjoys it? Why does she enjoy it?

The question leads to giving up. Tanja enjoys giving up.

Tanja, a twenty–nine–year–old master of literature and a young writer who has, with her brave debut short novel printed on less than a hundred pages three years ago, become one of the most promising literary hopes in ex–Yugoslavia, sits at an old desk which used to belong to her father, and now belongs to her, and no–one else, in front of an Apple notebook, trying to finalize a new collection of stories in which she testifies to small but crucial scenes from the lives of children, girls all across Europe and the Mediterranean. In her stories Tanja exposes the girls to different sorts of abuse, bare and visible, as well as those more subtle, discrete, invisible to the naked eye.

On the desk, next to the computer, there's a green lamp and a toy, a shabby plush pink–tailed lemur with eyelids drawn over its huge eyes. In the middle of the last story censorship occurs – Tanja simply stops. She isn't sure whether she wants to finish, whether she wants to give a final shape to this monster of a collection. Instead of writing, she just sits, wondering why she tortures those kids, wondering about the autonomy of literature, autonomy from what, from politics, life, society, from tabooed motifs, wondering about vanity, about whether it's a crime to deal with art, since where there's punishment, there must be a crime as well, wondering about the deep exile which friends and citizens take lightly as something voluntary and artistic, about the exile which follows her, but which she nonetheless doesn't find pleasing, wondering about artists who spend all their lives on subversiveness that remains utterly invisible, wondering whether invisible subversiveness is any fight at all, whether it's simply a certain manner of acceptance, wondering about the utilitarianism of art, from the theory of catharsis to the theory according to which cows produce more milk if they listen to Bach, wondering what dress to buy for the next summer, wondering whether to call Vladimir, who she hasn't heard from for two days, wondering whether she's put on weight. Wondering, but not writing. Leaving an unfinished sentence, she closes the laptop and rises.

The place where Tanja writes and reads is in fact a subterranean library built by her father, former university teacher and state official Dragan Milanović. It is in the basement of a house in the most beautiful part of the city, the house her parents left to Tanja two years ago, when they retired to a seaside cottage in Montenegro.

Tanja rises and repeats her ancient ritual which is part of her everyday life. Almost every day, since childhood,

Tanja would descend here, stand on a certain spot and close her eyes. This is how she would enter total darkness. With her fingers she would gently touch one of the books on the first shelf on the right and start walking slowly, feeling on her fingertips the familiar crossings from cover to cover, from plastic–coated cardboard to leather, from leather to fabric.

She does the same now: with her eyes closed she moves her hand across the book's micro–relief, walking like a confident blind person in the land of the blind, in the space where every single detail is completely familiar, whose every detail is part of her personality. Then she stops. She takes a randomly chosen book and opens it. Upon touching it, she recognizes one of the cheaper editions of Banjaluka's *Glas****. They are white, modestly produced books by Baudelaire, Valéry, Cavafy, de Góngora, John Donne, Akhmatova, Bryusov, Cavalcanti, Hebel, Swinburne and select others. She opens her eyes and, not looking at the title page, she recognizes the book *The Hunting of the Snark*, which the author, Lewis Carroll, sub–titled "An Agony in 8 Fits". She starts reading some verses devoted to a girl, from a randomly chosen page: *Girt with a boyish garb...*

Then she falls silent, but she keeps hearing her voice which seems to appear from all four sides... eager she wields her spade... to ask the tale... spright... delight, she is overwhelmed with words, and images, and this all forms a stereo experience of art, the world heritage. She ponders over the library she finds herself in. For her, it doesn't represent a Borgesian substitution for the world,

---

*   Serbian for "voice".

it's merely the place she knows best of all places in the world, somewhat otherworldly, and yet not a place of some other but of this world, her place. The only one where she anticipates good, despite all evils and follies which, in between the covers, sell themselves as pieces of wisdom, despite the false authorities upon which civilization has been built, despite commendations for the worst in man, she realizes these are exceptions, or at least simply parts of a sometimes necessarily manipulative culture, she feels good here, in an ideological and even more emotional sense, she feels good here, decent, safe.

Observing her colleagues at university, Tanja realizes that what is understood as classical education today can suck and drown one, strangle one. A victim starts to spend more time in the fifth century BC than in the present, falls in love with statues, theater arenas made of stone, iambs, trochees, and finally, without noticing it, she spends her life in an image of the world instead of the world itself. Fortunately, she has recognized such a danger lurking from these walls in a timely fashion, so that now all her books with the thoughts of Presocratics, her Ancient Greek tragedians, her Plato, Aristotle, Aesop, lyric poets, her Romans, her never forgotten Ovid, the universal guide and sycophant Virgil, her rare specimens of the Quran and the Bible, her One Thousand and One Nights... (her mind wanders off lightly here), so that she can finally love all these loves of hers in an objective, disinterested manner.

She understands them, but they also understand her and her need to live a contemporary life.

They co-exist.

Old history and literature textbooks are laid back here, it can easily be noticed that those who created them had a whole lifetime at their disposal in order to devote proper attention to them. Figure after figure from the cultural history of the ancient period, biographical data and anecdotes, extensive and always suspect portrayals of social milieus, bibliographies, and eventually reviews of works. Among those that have found their place here are almost unrecognizable tattered sheets of *The Tempest*, a perfect irony without which E. T. A. Hoffman could barely stand his imagination, the first Yugoslav editions of Machiavelli, More, Montaigne, Ronsard, Villon, Voltaire, Erasmus, Michelangelo's sonnets, which have wriggled coquettishly under her fingers so many times, which she has read so many times, which she has learned by heart. A small antiquarian Red Letter Library edition is also huddled in here, with collections of English romantic poets, printed in the late nineteenth and early twentieth century, then original editions of Soviet avant-garde poets (Mandelstam, her beloved Mandelstam, Khlebnikov, Zamyatin, passion, goose bumps when her eyes fall on them), her Philosophical library in the edition of Belgrade's *Culture*: Spinoza, Locke, de Chardin, Heidegger, even Schopenhauer, Nolit's *Between Reality and Dream*, Novalis and other works from the *Fantasies* edition and...

She'll stop. She'd better stop.

When she comes to think of it, the mentioned love seems not to be so indifferent. She'll stop, as she wouldn't like to name the entire catalog of riches that can be found here – and which were her father's gift to her, but the significance of these shelves doesn't lie only in ideas and images that are shown on them. Their importance is, in this case, rather personal. She has grown with these shelves and on these books. The first smell she became attached to was the smell of a library. All knowledge and experiences of this world with its autonomous rules were somehow implicit, ordinary. And when she would get out of this everyday temple, into what is called the real world, when she would see throngs pushing their way to get onto the public transport, resellers at the markets, hired hands waiting for any job in the cold, young mothers with three children, people in suits, business women, stylized adolescents, heavy metal fans, neo–punkers, hip-hoppers, she would assume that each one of them had a similar library of their own, that they had read at least as many books as her, that one couldn't and mustn't go outside without this. And, with this assumption, anything that they would do, any movement they would make, any detail in their appearance, ugly and trite though it may be, somehow had sense, it was still beautiful, friendly, easy to understand for her.

Later, maybe too late, she wonders, she understood she hadn't been right, and that the complexity and ambiguity of everyday life was only a figment of her imagination, and that the world was simpler, far simpler. This defeated her a little and made her set out in search of basic complexity in such niches of civilization as art and science. The search didn't have a logical conclusion, a genuine aim, but instead it became, in the Argonautic manner, a way of life, total surrender to which Tanja still resists well.

So, that's how Tanja would get lost in thoughts. She would stop writing halfway through a sentence. She would switch off her computer. Rise. Walk across her library. And then, abruptly, she would get sick and tired of everything. Locke and Khlebnikov and Shelley and Pound and Crnjanski and Borges and the lot. This happened more and more often, and she couldn't understand why. More and more often she had to leave this environment because she felt sick, physically sick. She would go up to the bathroom to refresh herself, to feel her body again.

Tanja takes off her clothes and gets into the shower. The shower is long and thorough – and it doesn't possess anything symbolic. She doesn't attempt to wash anything off her conscience or her past, she simply enjoys the perfect temperature of the water and the touch of her soft skin. Naked and wet, she enters the hallway and stands in front of the mirror. Here she is. Her twenty-nine ripe years, naked and wet, get out of the bathroom and stand in front of themselves. Now everything is the way it should be on this body, naked and wet, in this life, in this house.

Then she hears something, from below, something like counting:

Fif'y... fif'een... twen'y.

She goes back to the library and steps inside, taking care not to make noise with the squeaky door. She hides behind a shelf, peeks and sees herself as a girl in the opposite corner. She's about eight years old. She cannot tell this from her height, or face, but she can remember wearing exactly the same dress for her eighth birthday. Or was it the ninth?

She's a girl again. She's eight or nine. She observes herself. She feels the urge to address her little self, but she can no longer move. She wants to say hello, but the hand is still. The girl turns her head toward the wall and keeps on counting, quickly:

Twen'y–five, thi'ty, thi'ty–five, fo'ty, fo'ty–five, fifty, fif'y–five, sixty, six'y–five, se'nty, se'nty–five, eighty, ei'ty–five, ninety, nine'y–five, hundred!

Ready or not, here I come!

She shouts in a whisper, and then she turns very cautiously, taking into account the possibility that one of her friends hasn't hidden yet, but has instead, like a smart aleck, stood right behind her back, counting on her proverbial confusion and her own swiftness which would help her touch home base before Tanja even realizes what has happened. She hated it when the laws were thus broken and the play was rendered senseless. The rules had to be obeyed, otherwise everything would go to the dogs and collapse on our heads.

Fortunately, there was no–one nearby.

For a few moments, she glanced to the left, then to the right, thinking where to go. Hiding in the basement bathroom would be far too predictable, and Tanja doesn't socialize with dummies who do things on the spur of the moment and who do not pose serious challenges. She loved challenges, she loved tasks, she enjoyed pondering and riddle–solving. She remembers solving tasks from a math workbook for junior high school, one year, perhaps just before that eighth or ninth birthday, for forty–five days, which was a day short of the whole summer break, for eight hours a day, from eight till noon and from four till eight in the evening. Her aim was to solve them all in that period of time. But, page after page, the equations got more and more complex, the pleasure at relatively simple algorithmic problems was replaced by sweating over a more complex algebra and geometrical abstractions, so that, during the last month, she often skipped her lunch break and never rose. Still, she managed to carry out the mission, although she almost fainted while doing the last 'x'.

They certainly aren't in the bathroom. She finds herself concluding it isn't even worth searching there.

Perhaps in the wardrobe, under the old bed linen?

You must be a hero or a lunatic to hide there. That piece of furniture has hardly ever been opened. At least she hasn't ventured such a move ever since the moment she found a litter of naked baby mice wiggling and squeaking quietly, eerily. She finds herself, despite the fear, trying to cast a glance, a small, quick one. She approaches, turning around, so nobody could run up to her from the other side. She is in two minds. From the distance, as if she had a duty to touch something dirty, she reaches out her hands toward the loosened wooden handles. She makes a long pause before she suddenly grabs them and with a creaking sound opens the old double–door wardrobe which took up more space than was its due in this interior, like an old professor who constantly alludes to his immense authority.

The pause doesn't end the way she's planned. She's all stiff. The opening doesn't come easily to her. She merely knocks. Then she addresses those who were so clever to hide in the wardrobe:

May whoever is inside know they're found!

No sound at all.

Tanja's young, white face, almost with no signs of complexion, falls on the smooth, treated oak with the forehead. Then it starts sliding toward the floor. She pulls her favorite toy out of her big pocket, a small plush lemur, which she got, as the entire library later, from her father, she hugs it, and then clasps her small hands in a prayer in front of her forehead.

I pray to you, Holy Spirit, I pray to you. Please forgive me for wanting to open it. I pray to you, Holy Spirit, I pray to you. Please make it look like I didn't even think of it. I pray that no-one knows I had such a thought, that dad doesn't know, that mum doesn't know, that the books don't know, that the library doesn't know, that I don't know, that you don't know. I pray to you, Holy Spirit, I pray to you. I'm sorry.

Now she recalls, but previously she completely forgot all the prayers that occurred so often when she was a child and were based on the verbal utterance of any detail related to her wish. If she wished to get a new book, she had to explain its color and its size and the firmness of its covers in a prayer, if she prayed to suffer an unpleasantness without pain, to reconcile herself to it and enjoy it in her own freakish way, she would have to use such words that explain what her face would be like, what she would imagine while her eyes were closed, and suchlike.

Those prayers were neither self-sufficient nor addressed to some abstract omnipotence and omnipresence, they weren't uttered just for the sake of it, as they are uttered by many people, but they had two functions, as she thought back then.

The first was to address the Holy Spirit, who was in fact some sort of her personal god at the time. And she certainly had such a god. One, only for herself. He wasn't someone to control the situation and have in his hands a solution to any problem, but he was more of a friend, a trustworthy creature with good connections who could direct and push things rather than simply solve them.

The Holy Spirit got its missing corporeality in the small lemur.

The other function was, she realizes now, psychological. She would thus easily define her goals and know which directions to go, what to aim for. For this reason, her prayers had to be very concrete, as accurately described as possible.

She finds herself moving on.

Where are they?

Behind the shelf with Spanish writers?

There's a special place there, dad's place, hidden, with a reading armchair. Barely anyone ever enters it. She would hide there whenever she wanted not to be found, when she wanted to read something that wouldn't be recommended for her (a positive formulation of prohibition). She would gladly run up there.

No–one.

She stands in the center of the room. She begins to spin around quickly, more quickly, like a dervish. She stops after about ten circles and starts resolutely toward the sofa, as if she were absolutely certain that it was the right place to search for. No doubt.

The three–piece sofa has three forever–locked compartments under the seating section. Unlike the books which were merely not recommended, an explicit prohibition was put on opening these compartments. There must be someone there – they hid there because they know she mustn't peek inside on no account at all. They underestimated her. She's more courageous than that.

Self–confident, with no second thoughts about any possible uncertainties that might befall her due to this venture, she approaches a rarely opened drawer and takes three small keys which are supposed to be hidden from her. She lifts the heavy lid, unlocks the first compartment and finds a few folders on its bottom... (her father's papers, lectures, discarded lecture material, seminar papers in cobwebs). She opens another compartment, too. On its bottom, under two small pillows, she finds an old Colt pistol and a package of ammunition. She closes it, not thinking about what she's found there, but about what she's yet to find. At last, the opening of the third compartment brings a revelation.

I've found you!

She shouted.

You've hidden here.

Gloating, she speaks to the round female face that lies still in the half–darkness of the wooden box, she speaks to her own face:

You're mine!

Tanja looks at her little self emerging from the sofa with disheveled hair. She lifts to her face a piece of the broken mirror which was inside and threatens to her reflection:

You won't be there before me.

Carrying the mirror, she runs to the starting position and touches home base triumphantly:

Tag, you're it!

Then she looks again at her reflection, saying:

Your turn now.

She leans the mirror against the shelf and runs away. Tanja disappears from Tanja's view.

It's only a few moments before lame, imminent steps are heard. The girl runs out of her shelter, taking the first book she comes across on the shelf.

She sits on a step, whispering some lines from a randomly picked page:

Girt with a boyish garb for boyish task,
Eager she wields her spade: yet loves as well
Rest on a friendly knee, intent to ask
The tale he loves to tell.

Rude spirits of the seething outer strife,
Unmeet to read her pure and simple spright,
Deem, if you list, such hours a waste of life
Empty of all delight!

The door is opened by a man in his fifties, the graying professor Dragan Milanović. He's tired. Tired as she remembers him, as everybody remembers him.

But he has a mild voice:

Tanja!

The girl rises. She hugs him. She can smell stale tobacco and alcohol. Dad sits in his reading chair.

What are you reading? This again. My sweetheart. Give me a kiss.

The girl kisses her father on the cheek. Father kisses the girl on the neck, lifts her and places her in his lap. The girl is in her dad's lap. The girl is comfortable. The girl kisses her father, anew. Father puts his hands on Tanja's hips, on Tanja's thighs. He tucks his hand into her panties. They both shiver with pleasure.

Tanja looks at this eight–year–old girl, feeling scared, for the first time in her adult life she feels such an intense fear, not for what is about to happen, but because she's afraid to see what is about to happen. She suspects and realizes at the same time that she doesn't even recognize a hint of fear, of anything, on the girl's face.

Maybe for the first time in her adult life Tanja doesn't want to see now. She tries to close her eyes, but she can't, as if her eyes were open by force. In panic, she looks around for an object that would block the view. She attempts to push one of the shelves, but this venture is beyond her strength. Then she begins taking books out and making a wall of them. Quickly, quickly, she throws them all onto the floor, every single one, with no difference, foreign and domestic writers, classics and contemporaries, encyclopedias and novels, poets and philosophers, realists and postmodernists. When the shelter grows to about half a meter in height, she lies down and hides behind it. Finally, she cannot see. But she can hear sighs of pleasure. She can hear the words:

Do you love your daddy?

I do. I do.

Do you like this?

After this, silence. She feels nothing. A synesthetic experience of the mingling of the senses when we feel a strong fear has now boiled down to stench, the stench of books that haven't been taken from the shelves for long in the room unventilated for even longer.

Dare she peep?

Tanja peeks out.

Her father is no longer there.

He was there. An old, black tomcat in a black fur coat and a black fur cap on his head. There was some charm in his smile, some nonchalance, as in someone who possesses all the experiences of this world, who no longer craves anything and only wishes to exist.

– What, did you think I was dead? You don't read news?

There he was, Nicolae Ceauşescu.

– They've exhumed me today. Both me and Elena. In order to check if it was really us.

She realizes now that it's no smile at all, but a sneer of a hardcore cynic when it comes to anything that's human.

– Boors. Narrow minds. I've never been nor shall ever be interested in such. I'm only interested in people like you.

He stepped toward her, seemingly indecisive.

– Like you and your father.

Tanja rose, free of any anxiety, as if ready to confront the world, herself, like a symbol–image of the French Revolution.

– Yes, please. What would you like?

– I apologize. I haven't introduced myself. I am the Prince of the Underworld. Ha, what discrepancy there is between this romanticized name and my present appearance. Satan, Mephisto, as you wish, nice to meet you.

He introduced himself in a business manner and took off his fur cap with a slight bow.

– Satan?

Now she reacted scornfully, as if she'd seen a hysterical street prophet not leaving her alone at a busy crossroad or on public transport.

– You're looking at me as if I were a hysterical street prophet. I used to be that, as well. And I suggest that everybody try it, try to say something they believe in to people trapped in certain social circumstances. I got on a tram and, from one stop to another, I declaimed

in a suggestive voice a revolutionary call for boycott. I shouted insanely: Boycott!

He shouted in a voice that appeared to be coming from a deepest mine.

– Let's boycott the classical period! Myths, epics, tragedies, comedies and lyrics. All of this was given a much greater role in the later world than it was due. Let's boycott the Bible! The New Testament, the Old Testament, inspiring Job, apostles, Jesus and all virgin saints. Once and for all let's forget them and let them rest in peace.

Let's boycott the contemporary period! The current communication, readers, viewers, this alternate movement in several directions. It's treacherous and ephemeral, who knows what will remain of it.

Let's boycott language! The tale of fate, collective conscious and unconscious, nation and zaum. It's a manipulative structure and a pure lie.

Let's boycott man! Illusions of self–consciousness, society, civilization, concepts. All this is a smokescreen, and doesn't actually exist.

Let's boycott life! It's a miserable substitution for existence.

Everybody looked at me as you now. As soon as the tram came to a halt, they rushed out without a word. Like, they rush to work to get something done, and to school to learn something. I was dirty, barefoot. A maniac. I felt good. I felt good as much as they were uncomfortable... But I'm not here to tell you about my free time. I'm here on business.

Tanja stood in front of him, dignified, with her soul in a defensive position, pressed between her folded arms.

– What business?

– I've come to carry out a deal. I'm taking you with me.

– Where are you taking me?

– You aren't stupid. To Hell.

She laughed almost genuinely now.

– Wait a minute. I don't know who you are, nor why you are dressed like a dictator, nor what you want from me. You really are a maniac. Is this invitation to Hell merely an inapt sort of invitation to sex? I'll call the police.

– Tanja, it's a bit more complex than that. Let's go.

– I'm not going anywhere.

– Come on. You have to.

– Of course, I don't have to. Leave me alone!

He came close to her, caught her under the arm and began to pull her.

– Hey, you jerk! Leave me alone! Heeeelp!

– I can't leave you alone. I've finally come for what's mine and this is exactly what I'll get.

– What are you talking about?

– Wait, I'll show you.

He held her hand gently, but his suggestiveness was so pronounced that Tanja immediately started in the direction he pulled her, to her father's forbidden cupboard. He opened it and showed Tanja an old sheet of paper which he pulled from below a heap of different manuscripts.

– What does it say here?

Tanja reads the last sentence:

– I hereby oblige myself that my daughter, Tanja Milanović, shall be Your possession starting from the day I die and that you may take her to Hell where you can keep her for ever and ever. The execution of the contract shall automatically come into force upon determining the contractual terms. I waive the right to appeal.

– Yes. And... whose signature is this?

– My father's.

– That's right. There's also a witness's signature, to prevent any...

– Mum?

– There, now you can see well. Come with me.

– I've had enough of this. What nonsense. How could he oblige himself that I would become someone's property? What's this all about? And, my father is still alive!

– What, they didn't tell you?! Huh, I don't like breaking such news. The old professor passed away this morning, while he was swimming. What does he think, that he can swim three kilometers along a rocky shore in his seventies? He's always overestimated himself.

– Passed away?

– Yes. I'm sorry, but let's go back to the contract now. It is all well stated. He sold your soul for a couple of years...

– ... Satan shall be obliged to provide two decades of lawless life to his client...

She read out loud the main item of the contract, and the bully finished off.

– ... and with no fear of punishment.

– That's none of my business! I'm not my father. Leave me alone. Don't pull me! You maniac. Help!

With the last word, enriched with a devotional tone, new uninvited guests showed up in this room. They ran into the library in a very organized fashion, formed a line, and then stood to attention. There were about twenty naked girls aged between six and fifteen years old, of different looks and races. As if she knew them from somewhere, from her invented memories, from her stories. They were Julia and Almira and Alexandra and Samia and Zeinab and Monika and Fausta and all the other girls of hers, and then her again, as a small child. They had huge black eyes, a lemur's eyes.

– Oho, my faithful army. Uninvited? How come you're here? I think I don't need your help here. Tanja, let me introduce them, these are lemurs, part of my big army. They belong to the elite division which operates in the central part of my military area – Europe, the Mediterranean and the Middle East. You know, according to Mackinder's heartland geopolitical theory, who owns one essentially strategic region will possess the entire world. This division of my proud army will bring me global domination. Isn't that so, troops?

Like in a choir, lemur–girls addressed Satan:

– Leave her alone! You have no claim to her.

The Lord of Hell glanced at them sternly, but sympathetically, like at brats unaware of their doings.

– Oho, a coup? What kind of rebellion is this?

– Leave her alone. We can no longer look at young contorted faces. We've decided to rebel. We're taking her to meet her Maker. She's going with us, to Heaven.

– Ha–ha, you don't know what you're talking about. Be good, calm down. I have a contract.

– It's null and void...

– She's mine!

He put his arms tightly round her waist, lifted her and ran toward the girls. He managed to break through the cordon, but he didn't reach far. They already caught up with him on the stairs leading to the living room. They caught Tanja by the leg and started pulling her toward themselves. Satan didn't give in. They stretched the helpless body. He was strong, very strong, but the girls were too many. The entire commotion lasted long, perhaps ten, fifteen minutes, when, at one moment of terrible noise and neglect, Tanja managed to get away both from the angel's and the devil's hands.

– *I am nobody's! Neither yours! Nor yours! Nor...*

She ran back to the library, took the Colt from the middle compartment, locked herself and hid again behind a small heap of books.

When she woke up the next morning, she could see a compelling scene: Aeschylus and Euripides and Sophocles, Cervantes, Rabelais and Grimmelshausen, Tolstoy, Flaubert, Huysmans and Gide, Dostoyevsky, Mann, Musil, Vuk and Branko and Dučić, Rastko, Andrić and Krleža... and Ben and Trakl and Brecht... and Rilke and Pound and Brodsky and Mandelstam... Céline and Hamsun and Nabokov... all those men piled up on the floor, between her legs, around her and below her, pressed tight at the Thermopylae Pass, motionless and bleeding, wounded, to death, one would say.

She's got her period. Her blood has soaked the pages of Goethe's *Faust* which stuck to her body as a frightened animal. A small clot has found its place on the back cover, and Tanja's corporeality has reached all the way to the famous line: "The Eternal Feminine draws us on high"*.

She felt good. As if this bloodshed of classics, and those yet to become such, was her revenge for some

---

* Translated by *Luke, David (1987). Faust, Part One. Oxford: Oxford University Press.*

wrong done to her, for a crime she didn't even remember, she didn't want to remember, which might never have happened, which never happened. After all, if anything had happened, they were the culprits, those quiet onlookers, silent, so silent witnesses.

She changed her clothes and, as every morning, went to Weimar Café, which is within easy reach of her house.

The owner of this place is a likeable middle–aged German who married in Belgrade and brought some of his habits over here. One of them is the purchase of all issues of the *Landleben* magazine. Tanja often leafs through the plastic–coated pages of these luxury issues. On them, she finds idyllically portrayed houses and cottages in the countryside, rustically furnished rooms enriched with state–of–the–art technology, happy people sitting in their yard next to a small, probably artificial lake. Their faces shriek with tranquility, a religious serenity achieved by their Protestant attitude to work, careful and persistent drudgery at any detail of their lives and living space. The colors that dominate the pages are light blue and white, then different shades of the natural tree colors – walnut, oak, beech and other materials unknown to her. Until recently abandoned and old, but now with newborn love and the most modern materials and techniques refurbished railway stations, porches, summer houses, stables, carriages, attics, great–grandmothers' kitchens, granddads' sofas exude warmness and discretion from the posters.

Now Tanja held an issue published near the end of last fall, in which entire four pages were devoted to Kristian Adler, former manager for new investments in a big Frankfurt–based company, who decided, almost twenty years ago, to move from Frankfurt to his parents' village, and asked a relative from that area to find him a good offer for an old countryside house. He found one at an excellent price, but instead of a regular facility, he found a small countryside church made of stone and wood which had long been replaced with a newer one, and was now left without its sheep and shepherd.

Kristian had enough of metropolitan hysteria, rude clients and employers, everyday expectations and intensity which surpassed his physical and emotional capabilities. Still, he didn't lose his entrepreneurial and innovative spirit, so he decided to rename the home of God to his own home. During the last two decades he has replaced almost everything in this facility. The tin on the roof was replaced with new tin on the roof. The sky blue was painted over with new sky blue. The dilapidated windows were replaced with new windows of the same shape. Then he procured some furniture that utterly fitted the ambience. He arranged every detail carefully and meticulously. Photographs illustrated the entire process. The old church could be seen gradually turning into a new home.

Kristian stood in front of his house, in his dungarees, smiling.

Kristian sat on the sofa in his house, with tea before himself, smiling.

Kristian played with his retriever in the backyard, smiling.

Kristian hugged his smiling wife, smiling.

Kristian spoke and the journalist took notes about how he'd decided to leave the city for somewhere inland.

Kristian said he knew straightaway that that was it, when he cast a look at the former place of worship.

Kristian stated that his marriage could be said to have been saved by moving to the countryside.

Kristian said he was happy with his decision.

It's no use coming back, Tanja thought. You can't return, even somewhere you've never been.

It's no use. You have to move on.

Any time when the café isn't crowded, as is the case now, Tanja sits at the table next to the wall with paintings. Whenever she manages to seat herself on her favorite chair, and here every chair is unique, every one of them has a particular shape, different color and belongs to a different world, above her head is a small fish tank. It's actually a glass bowl with the radius of not more than twenty-five centimeters, which hangs from one of the low ceiling boards with some uninspiring tourist souvenirs of the owner and his family from various world destinations. Mister Joschka Fischer, an ungroomed fish whose witty name was proudly written on the table below his residence, lived in that hanging, hyper-transparent, cramped water world, until yesterday.

Today the fish tank is empty, and the following is written in front of the name, in black felt-tip pen: R. I. P.

She's used to Joschka and now she wonders for a long while whether to ask the owner what's happened to him or not, how he passed away. She won't, though. Some doors can be left closed. Some questions can be left unanswered. Some questions are simply stupid and pathetic.

Tanja's phone rings. The name *Mum* shows on the display. Mum rarely calls her, and when she does, she only calls her on the home number. Tanja knows her mother's calling because something's happened to her father.

Tanja doesn't answer.
Tanja switches the phone to silent mode.
Tanja keeps on leafing through the magazine.

ABOUT THE AUTHOR

Bojan Babić was born in Belgrade in 1977. He studied at the Department of Serbian and World Literature at the Faculty of Philology, in Belgrade, and later gained a Master's degree from the same department. Before commencing his studies in Serbian and World Literature, he was a singer in a little-known heavy metal/grunge band. Over the last ten years, he has worked as a prolific and acclaimed copywriter and associate creative director at a big advertising agency, winning numerous awards.

Bojan Babić began writing in the middle of the last decade of the twentieth century (when the war in the former Yugoslavia was raging), in his teenage years and early twenties. In that period, he wrote and published two books: *Noises in prose* – hermetic poetry with "delicate language tendencies and surreal stoicism in a world with no hope", and *PLI-PLI*, a book of flash-fiction. What motivated him to start writing was an inability to cope with the situation of absolute violence and destruction all around him, on the one hand, and his youthful fascination with the poets of the French, German and Soviet avant-garde, on the other. Those first attempts thus came about as a result of activism and escapism at the same time.

Ever since he took his first steps in writing, he has been concerned by questions that are still dominant themes in his literature today: irreparable harm, a loss of faith in the idea that things can get any better, a pessimism about history and civilization which, over time, turns into anthropopessimism, a loss of belief in human kind. These and many other questions have, in various ways, from various perspectives and using various poetic strategies, arisen in Babic's books. With no definite answer.

As one critic wrote of Babic's novel *Inhuman comedy*, realistic prose seems too feeble and naïve to describe the unbelievable reality that is happening to us, hence Babic uses surreal tactics to talk about it. If one had to come up with a name for it, it would be called dystopic surreal realism, in which he always adds a pinch of dark humor, irony and an oneiric atmosphere. Critics have compared his prose to that of Don DeLillo, Boris Vian and Roberto Bolanjo.

Babic won an award from the Borislav Pekić Foundation in 2011. His novel *Illegal Parnassus*, published in 2013, was shortlisted for the biggest national literary award, the *NIN prize*; it was also shortlisted for the biggest regional award (for Bosnia and Herzegovina, Montenegro, Croatia and Serbia) – the *Meša Selimović prize*. Critics have reacted very strongly to his last three novels. He has appeared as a guest teacher in several creative writing schools.

He has had prose, poetry and essays published in a large number of magazines and anthologies in Serbia and abroad.

- *A History of Belarus* by Lubov Bazan
- *Children's Fashion of the Russian Empire* by Alexander Vasiliev
- *Empire of Corruption: The Russian National Pastime* by Vladimir Soloviev
- *Heroes of the 90s: People and Money. The Modern History of Russian Capitalism* by Alexander Solovev, Vladislav Dorofeev and Valeria Bashkirova
- *Fifty Highlights from the Russian Literature* (Dutch Edition) by Maarten Tengbergen
- *Bajesvolk* (Dutch Edition) by Michail Chodorkovsky
- *Dagboek van Keizerin Alexandra* (Dutch Edition)
- *Myths about Russia* by Vladimir Medinskiy
- *Boris Yeltsin: The Decade that Shook the World* by Boris Minaev
- *A Man Of Change: A study of the political life of Boris Yeltsin*
- *Sberbank: The Rebirth of Russia's Financial Giant* by Evgeny Karasyuk
- *To Get Ukraine* by Oleksandr Shyshko
- *Asystole* by Oleg Pavlov
- *Gnedich* by Maria Rybakova
- *Marina Tsvetaeva: The Essential Poetry*
- *Multiple Personalities* by Tatyana Shcherbina
- *The Investigator* by Margarita Khemlin
- *The Exile* by Zinaida Tulub
- *Leo Tolstoy: Flight from Paradise* by Pavel Basinsky
- *Moscow in the 1930* by Natalia Gromova
- *Laurus* (Dutch edition) by Evgenij Vodolazkin
- *Prisoner* by Anna Nemzer
- *The Crime of Chernobyl: The Nuclear Goulag* by Wladimir Tchertkoff
- *Alpine Ballad* by Vasil Bykau
- *The Complete Correspondence of Hryhory Skovoroda*
- *The Tale of Aypi* by Ak Welsapar
- *Selected Poems* by Lydia Grigorieva
- *The Fantastic Worlds of Yuri Vynnychuk*
- *The Garden of Divine Songs and Collected Poetry of Hryhory Skovoroda*
- *Adventures in the Slavic Kitchen: A Book of Essays with Recipes* by Igor Klekh
- *Seven Signs of the Lion* by Michael M. Naydan

- *Forefathers' Eve* by Adam Mickiewicz
- *One-Two* by Igor Eliseev
- *Girls, be Good* by Bojan Babić
- *Time of the Octopus* by Anatoly Kucherena
- *The Grand Harmony* by Bohdan Ihor Antonych
- *The Selected Lyric Poetry Of Maksym Rylsky*
- *The Shining Light* by Galymkair Mutanov
- *The Frontier: 28 Contemporary Ukrainian Poets - An Anthology*
- *Acropolis: The Wawel Plays* by Stanisław Wyspiański
- *Contours of the City* by Attyla Mohylny
- *Conversations Before Silence: The Selected Poetry of Oles Ilchenko*
- *The Secret History of my Sojourn in Russia* by Jaroslav Hašek
- *Mirror Sand: An Anthology of Russian Short Poems*
- *Maybe We're Leaving* by Jan Balaban
- *Death of the Snake Catcher* by Ak Welsapar
- *A Brown Man in Russia* by Vijay Menon
- *Hard Times* by Ostap Vyshnia
- *The Flying Dutchman* by Anatoly Kudryavitsky
- *Nikolai Gumilev's Africa* by Nikolai Gumilev
- *Combustions* by Srđan Srdić
- *The Sonnets* by Adam Mickiewicz
- *Dramatic Works* by Zygmunt Krasiński
- *Four Plays* by Juliusz Słowacki
- *Little Zinnobers* by Elena Chizhova
- *We Are Building Capitalism! Moscow in Transition 1992-1997* by Robert Stephenson
- *The Nuremberg Trials* by Alexander Zvyagintsev
- *The Hemingway Game* by Evgeni Grishkovets
- *A Flame Out at Sea* by Dmitry Novikov
- *Jesus' Cat* by Grig
- *Want a Baby and Other Plays* by Sergei Tretyakov
- *Mikhail Bulgakov: The Life and Times* by Marietta Chudakova
- *Leonardo's Handwriting* by Dina Rubina
- *A Burglar of the Better Sort* by Tytus Czyżewski
- *The Mouseiad and other Mock Epics* by Ignacy Krasicki
- *Ravens before Noah* by Susanna Harutyunyan

- *An English Queen and Stalingrad* by Natalia Kulishenko
- *Point Zero* by Narek Malian
- *Absolute Zero* by Artem Chekh
- *Olanda* by Rafał Wojasiński
- *Robinsons* by Aram Pachyan
- *The Monastery* by Zakhar Prilepin
- *The Selected Poetry of Bohdan Rubchak: Songs of Love, Songs of Death, Songs of the Moon*
- *Mebet* by Alexander Grigorenko
- *The Orchestra* by Vladimir Gonik
- *Everyday Stories* by Mima Mihajlović
- *Slavdom* by Ľudovít Štúr
- *The Code of Civilization* by Vyacheslav Nikonov
- *Where Was the Angel Going?* by Jan Balaban
- *De Zwarte Kip* (Dutch Edition) by Antoni Pogorelski
- *Głosy / Voices* by Jan Polkowski
- *Sergei Tretyakov: A Revolutionary Writer in Stalin's Russia* by Robert Leach
- *Opstand* (Dutch Edition) by Władysław Reymont
- *Dramatic Works* by Cyprian Kamil Norwid
- *Children's First Book of Chess* by Natalie Shevando and Matthew McMillion
- *Precursor* by Vasyl Shevchuk
- *The Vow: A Requiem for the Fifties* by Jiří Kratochvil
- *De Bibliothecaris* (Dutch edition) by Mikhail Jelizarov
- *Subterranean Fire* by Natalka Bilotserkivets
- *Vladimir Vysotsky: Selected Works*
- *Behind the Silk Curtain* by Gulistan Khamzayeva
- *The Village Teacher and Other Stories* by Theodore Odrach
- *Duel* by Borys Antonenko-Davydovych
- *War Poems* by Alexander Korotko
- *Ballads and Romances* by Adam Mickiewicz
- *The Revolt of the Animals* by Wladyslaw Reymont
- *Poems about my Psychiatrist* by Andrzej Kotański
- *Liza's Waterfall: The hidden story of a Russian feminist* by Pavel Basinsky
- *Biography of Sergei Prokofiev* by Igor Vishnevetsky

More coming ...

www.ingramcontent.com/pod-product-compliance
Lightning Source LLC
Chambersburg PA
CBHW032028180726
48284CB00008B/2528